The Summer of Telling Tales

'I loved *The Summer of Telling Tales*
– it's truly gripping and you care
desperately about both sisters.'
Jacqueline Wilson

'Fans of Cathy Cassidy will love
this absorbing tale of families and loyalty.'
The Bookseller

'I thoroughly enjoyed this perceptive, pacy story.'
Miriam Halahmy, author of *Hidden*

PRAISE FOR LAURA SUMMERS

Desperate Measures

Winner of the AMI Literature Award
Nominated for the Carnegie Medal
Longlisted for the Branford Boase Award
Shortlisted for the Waterstone's Children's Book Prize

'An exciting adventure with plenty of drama
and humour . . . Thought-provoking and moving.'
Books for Keeps

'A fabulous book . . . incredibly poignant.'
Birmingham Post

'The underlying issues do not overpower this story of
family loyalties and friendship.'
School Librarian

Heartbeat Away

'A mystery with a hint of the paranormal . . .
Laura Summers proves she's
a distinctive and original voice.'
The Bookseller

'A great book, with a totally original storyline.'
Crème Magazine

LAURA SUMMERS

The Summer of Telling Tales

PICCADILLY PRESS · LONDON

First published in Great Britain in 2013
by Piccadilly Press
A Templar/Bonnier publishing company
Deepdene Lodge, Deepdene Avenue, Dorking, Surrey, RH5 4AT
www.piccadillypress.co.uk

ISBN: 978 1 84812 231 4 (paperback)

1 3 5 7 9 10 8 6 4 2

Printed and bound by CPI Group (UK) Ltd, Croydon, CR0 4YY
Cover design by Simon Davis

Dedicated to my mother,
Pamela Ruth Cranfield
23rd September 1929 – 12th September 2012

Chapter 1

Ellie

'Just promise me you won't say a word to anyone,' Mum whispers, as Grace and I leave for school.

'I won't,' I tell her. 'It's OK, Mum.'

She doesn't need to say any more. I'd rather share a picnic with flesh-eating zombies than tell anyone what happens at home.

She smiles that big smile as she gently closes the front door, so she stays on my mind all day long. I see her in every lesson, at lunchtime as I eat my cheese and jam sarnies, and even in assembly while Mrs Stone rants on about inappropriate behaviour in the corridors. I keep going over and over what happened last night, but all the time I'm on autopilot, happy-smiley-happy, pretending to everyone that it's just another ordinary day.

By the time school finishes, my face is aching and my head's thumping, so I find Grace and we hurry along the pavement, weaving our way around bunches of kids chatting and laughing as they stroll home.

'She'll be OK, won't she?' I ask Grace again. She nods but speeds up, so now I'm jogging to keep up. I'd begged Mum to let us stay home today but she'd said we had to go in like normal.

'Hey, Ellie, wait!' I hear a voice call from down the street.

It's Lauren. She's new in my class, funny and friendly and really popular already. Just the sort of girl I'd love to be instead of me. As she crosses the road and heads towards us, I can feel Grace tugging my sleeve, but it's too late now. I can't pretend I haven't heard her.

'Can I come round yours for a while?' she asks, catching us up.

I force a smile to mirror hers. 'Maybe tomorrow,' I say with a lame shrug.

'You said that last time,' Lauren replies. She turns to Grace. 'You Ellie's sister then?' she asks, her eyes wide.

She isn't expecting this tall, stunning princess, with tumbling silky hair, cornflower-blue eyes and china-smooth skin. Lauren obviously thought my sister would be my clone – another instantly forgettable, snub-nosed kid with a generous sprinkling of spots – just a year older and a centimetre or two taller than me. Nothing special and definitely not a princess – more like the slave who empties the bins.

Lauren's friendliness is wasted on Grace. She ignores her, darts me an urgent look, then turns to go. I'm cringing all over. Why can't she just speak, for goodness' sake? It's so embarrassing. One word would do – 'yes', 'no', 'hello' . . . whatever.

'Yeah, that's Grace,' I quickly blurt out, not wanting to explain right now that my sister doesn't talk to anyone except me. 'Sorry. Gotta go.'

Lauren is staring at me curiously. I want to get away before she asks any more awkward questions.

'What's up?'

'Nothing,' I say with a laugh. 'Dad's taking us out for pizza when we get home.'

'Lucky thing!' Lauren calls after me. 'Wish my dad was like yours!'

I don't answer but grin and give her a wave.

'What did you say that for?' Grace asks fiercely, as we turn the corner.

'I don't know . . . last time . . . last time he was sorry . . . I just thought . . . '

Maybe everything *is* my fault, like he says. If I was quiet like Grace, or good at something and wasn't such a pain, I wouldn't stress him out all the time.

Grace glances at me and her face softens. 'Lauren'll stop asking soon,' she says.

And I'm angry and sad and relieved all rolled into one because I know she's right. They all stop asking after a while.

Chapter 2

Grace

Mulberry Grove. Our road. An exclusive cul-de-sac, Dad says. All the houses look the same, painted white with mock black beams, red tiled roofs and heavy net curtains in the front windows so no one can see in.

'Grace, don't you ever wonder what it would be like if things were different?' There's a wobble in Ellie's voice.

'No point.' My eyes zigzag across the street.

Number 3 – Mr and Mrs Lawn-Trimmed-With-Nail-Scissors.

Number 4 – Mrs Six Cats.

Number 5 – Mr Sad-Gnomes.

Number 6 –

'But wouldn't it be amazing if we were other people, living completely different lives?' she insists.

Why be anyone else? Other people are the problem.

Keep walking. Keep counting.

Number 8 – House for sale.

Number 9 –

'Oh, come on, Grace, tell me who would you be and

4

where?' She gabbles on. 'Anyone you want and anywhere you like.'

'OK, still me – on a desert island.' My stomach's churning, big time.

Ignore it.

Number 9 – Honeysuckle Cottage (who are they kidding?).

'Well you wouldn't catch me being me!' Ellie says with a nervous snort. 'I'd be someone glamorous, and obviously gob-smackingly beautiful, like a film star. And I'd swan around all day in my massive mansion, relaxing in my heart-shaped pool with ice cream sundaes lined up all around the edge.'

I've heard it all before. Ellie could talk for England. It's all right for some. I brought home my GCSE options form last week. Dad's decided my future's in dentistry – there's money in teeth. He ticked triple science, so I have to drop art. But I want to be a fashion designer and the thought of poking around in other people's mouths makes me want to puke. I made a list of what to say – put down everything. Then, standing in front of him, the words jammed up in my throat. In the end I had to swallow them all down, and they rolled around inside me like leftover school burgers.

And that's the feeling now. I've had it all day – right from when I woke up and tried not to remember last night. Must have looked bad as even Mrs Evans asked me in my violin lesson if everything was OK. I really wanted to tell her 'no' but I couldn't. Couldn't even get that one little word past the invisible gag over my mouth. Then my palms started sweating and I felt my face going red, so I just nodded and got stuck into my violin piece. By the time I'd finished, she'd forgotten she'd asked, offered me a boiled sweet and started going on about putting me in for some big music competition. I didn't care, but I knew Dad would be pleased if I won something.

And now we're here.

Number 14 – Home Sweet Home.

Push open the gate. Do it.

My hand's shaking slightly. We scurry up the path neatly edged with clumps of lavender, past the rose bushes growing in the funny little dip in the middle of the lawn where Ellie pretends a vampire's buried, and make our way around the side of the house to the kitchen door.

Stop and listen.

It's dead quiet until a car door slams and we both jump, but it's only Mr Kensell from next door, who waves and smiles. He's wearing a grey suit and carrying a book under his arm. He and Dad are good friends.

'Hi, girls!' he calls, smoothing a hand across the top of his head as the wind blows his comb-over up into the air. 'Tell your dad the next Neighbourhood Watch meeting is Monday evening, will you?'

I nod and Ellie calls 'OK' but then we both freeze as he comes over and leans across the fence.

'Oh and give him this for me, will you?' he adds, handing me a big glossy book about birds. 'Tell him thanks; it was very kind of him to lend me it. Very kind indeed.'

He walks back to his house, humming. Dad gets on well with all our neighbours. Even Mr Sad-Gnomes. Mr Kensell's son Danny, who doesn't have a comb-over yet but is in training for one, told Ellie that Dad was a 'top bloke' the other day.

I turn the handle of the kitchen door and push it open.

S-l-o-w-l-y.

The black and white floor tiles are spotless. The queasy feeling gets stronger. I slip off my shoes and place them where we're supposed to: one tile's width away from the kitchen wall.

'Mum?' Ellie calls. No answer. The broken plates from last night have been swept up and binned. Everything's neat and tidy. Not a fork or a dish mop out of place. Bruno looks up, but when he clocks it's only us, he carries on licking invisible drops of sauce from the floor, his tail wagging.

'Mum!' Ellie calls louder, opening the door to the hall, 'You OK?'

There's a muffled noise from upstairs. We run up to find her bending over an open suitcase in her and Dad's bedroom. She's not wearing one of her usual high-necked, long-sleeved blouses and smart trousers but an old white T-shirt and jeans. The side of her neck is bruised with angry purple and black blotches.

She looks up and smiles.

Ellie bursts into tears, runs over and hugs her tightly. Mum winces in pain but shushes Ellie and smoothes her hair like she's the one who's been hurt.

'We've only got ten minutes,' she says. 'Pack what you want to keep most. We're leaving.'

Chapter 3

Ellie

'Are we going to Auntie Anna's?' I ask wide-eyed. Dad doesn't allow Mum to see her sister. Says she's a bad influence and a lot of other much ruder things too.

Mum shakes her head. 'No, she doesn't know anything about this.'

'Then where?'

Mum shrugs. 'Away. Somewhere we can't be found.' She glances nervously at her watch then hands us a large canvas bag each. They're the ones we pack full of stuff when we're going on holiday.

'We can't take much,' she tells us, 'only what we can fit in the car. I've got some clothes, your sleeping bags and I've made some sandwiches for tea.'

It's as if we're going on an outing.

'What about Bruno?' I ask.

Mum looks at us and pulls a face.

'We can't leave Bruno, Mum!' I protest. 'We just can't!'

She puts her arm around me. 'I'm really sorry. He'll be OK,' she says gently. 'Girls, we've got to hurry. Your dad —'

Out of the blue, the phone suddenly rings. We all recognise the number on the display and exchange terrified glances. Mum reaches over the bedside table and slowly picks up the receiver.

'Hi, Adam,' she says, her voice calm but her eyes wide with fear.

It's Dad checking up. He rings Mum at random times from work every day to find out what she's doing and make sure she's not gone out without his say-so.

Mum waves us out of the bedroom and tells him she's just about to start cooking tea: steak and onion pie made from scratch, his favourite. I'm frightened that he might be able to hear her shaking but somehow she keeps her cool and tells him about the flowers she's planted in the garden today.

'He's going to go ballistic when he gets home and finds we're not here,' I whisper to Grace, who doesn't reply.

I go into my room, change quickly out of my school uniform into my jeans and a T-shirt then look around at all my stuff. I don't know where to start. What do I take? What do I leave?

Downstairs I can hear Bruno whimpering to be let out of the kitchen. Dad doesn't allow him anywhere else in the house but sometimes Grace and I secretly let him out and play with him in the sitting room when Dad's at work. Once we forgot to check for dog hair and Dad found out. He tied Bruno up outside for a week to teach him a lesson. It was last January and freezing cold. Even though Grace and I both begged him, he wouldn't let him in.

I glance round my room again and take a deep breath. I know now exactly what I want to take.

Chapter 4

Grace

No time for lists.

I hunt in my wardrobe for the brown paper carrier bag hidden at the back.

Got it.

Carefully, I take out the patchwork quilt inside. Dad has no idea that I rescued it the morning after he threw it in the dustbin, months ago, and it's lain secretly in here ever since. I haven't even dared to show Mum or Ellie, in case he finds out.

Gran made it for Mum's birthday last year. A few of the patches have tiny holes where they've been nibbled by moths and some pieces are so old and have been washed so many times they've faded loads, but the whole thing is still so breathtakingly beautiful that even now I don't understand why Dad hated it . . . unless it was Mum's reaction that did it.

He used to call Gran an interfering old bag. Made it clear that she wasn't welcome here, so, like Auntie Anna, we hardly ever saw her, although she always sent cards and parcels at birthdays and Christmas.

When Mum unwrapped Gran's parcel, her face lit up for a

split second. She immediately pulled down the shutters but a telltale spark still flickered in her eyes and Dad saw how much she loved it. We did too. It's a blast of colours.

Sky blue.

Cherry.

Lemon.

Emerald.

Rose pink.

Tangerine.

Lilac.

Ruby.

Gold.

Turquoise.

Like a garden full of flowers, Ellie insisted, seconds before Dad snatched it from Mum's hands.

'I'm not having this tatty rubbish in my house!' he said angrily, rolling it into a bundle. 'Who in their right mind would give someone a load of old rags for their birthday?'

Ellie protested. Mum just looked down and didn't say a word. Dad carried it into the kitchen and a few seconds later we heard fabric ripping. Ellie started crying. She tried to rush out to stop him but Mum held on to her tightly. 'It doesn't matter,' she kept saying. 'It doesn't matter.'

The following evening he came home from work with a quilt cover he'd bought from a posh department store near his office. Real Chinese silk, hand-embroidered with dragons intertwined in black and red. Cost him an arm and a leg but would be an heirloom, he told us, something for Mum to keep forever. She said it was beautiful. She stroked the silk but the spark was gone from her eyes.

No one mentioned Gran's present again but a few days later I went on a school trip to a museum, and between the dinosaur bones and iron-age tools they had an exhibition of quilts. Everyone else just whizzed past them as a rumour had gone round about a gruesome severed head on display, but I hung back and read all the little display cards on the quilts.

The more I read, the more I learnt. Quilts weren't just made by people with time on their hands; they were a way of communicating stuff that couldn't be said out loud. Wives sewed insults about their domineering husbands, and servants dished the dirt on the masters and mistresses. There were political messages, love letters, even rude jokes.

There were 'freedom quilts' too. American slaves used to send secret messages to each other by stitching symbols onto their quilts. Then they'd hang them out of windows or on washing lines and other escaping slaves would know there was a safe house or help waiting for them.

Back home, I got to thinking that maybe Gran was sending Mum more than just a load of patches of fabric sewn together. Maybe she was sending a coded message. So when Dad wasn't here, I'd take out the pieces of torn quilt and check to see if there were any mysterious symbols that I could translate. I never found anything.

But then something dawned on me. Every single scrap of the quilt had belonged to either Gran, Grandad, Mum or Auntie Anna, and all had been cut from clothes they'd once worn, so each piece had a story to it. I realised then that Gran's quilt was full of tales that Ellie and I aren't allowed to hear any more. And that was Gran's secret message. She was telling us not to forget.

So I started to mend the quilt, piece by piece, when Dad was out. I had to be careful and sew only a strip or two at a time just in case he came home unexpectedly. Once I got so involved there were pieces strewn all over my bedroom floor and I only just bundled them all away before he came in.

Eventually, after a few weeks, it was all sewn back together; not as neatly as Gran's work, because she was a professional seamstress when she was younger, but I learnt as I stitched and didn't do a bad job in the end. I still didn't dare show Mum the quilt but from then on I started making my own clothes, buying stuff from charity shops, chopping and mixing and sewing bits back together, and adding ribbon, beads or lace to create new dresses that I know Gran would have loved too.

She died a few months later. At the funeral Mum couldn't stop crying. Dad spoke to the vicar after the service and told him Gran would be sadly missed. The vicar patted his arm and whispered comforting words. We didn't go to Auntie Anna's afterwards with everyone else. Dad said Mum was too upset and needed to go home. When we got back, she made dinner and he watched a documentary about golden eagles.

I fold the quilt, put it back in the brown paper carrier, then carefully place it inside my canvas bag under my violin case.

Not much room left now.

I wrap my shell earrings and necklace in the pieces of dress I'm making, then gently cram that down one side of the bag and Gran's old wooden needlework box packed with all my sewing stuff down the other.

Must have paper and a couple of pens for my lists.

They go in last. I change into my favourite long flowery dress, the one Dad says makes me look like a bag lady, then pull my chunky raspberry-coloured jumper over the top for warmth. I glance at the piece of paper sellotaped to the inside of the wardrobe door, listing all the violin music and scales I'm practising at the moment.

'Ellie. Grace. We've got to leave now,' Mum calls softly from downstairs.

I throw my uniform into the wardrobe, tuck my purse into my dress pocket and grab my bag.

I take one final glance around my bedroom, with its heavy brass-trimmed furniture and those horrible, stiff, navy blue curtains, then hurry out.

Chapter 5

Ellie

Mum's car is in the garage. She's allowed to use it for emergencies and on Fridays for the food shopping. On Saturday mornings, she gives Dad all the receipts and change, then the next Friday morning, after he's had the time to check it all through, he gives her enough money to buy everything for the following week. Because he's the one earning the wage, he says he should be the one who decides how it's spent.

About two years ago, Auntie Anna got Mum an interview for a part-time job in a florist's so she could have her own money but when Dad found out where she'd been, and that she'd got the job, he hit the roof and said he didn't work all hours so his wife could go out like a skivvy.

Later that night, I could still hear their voices in the kitchen, arguing. It was scary so I got out of bed and went down, pretending I wanted a glass of water just to make them stop, but it didn't work. In the morning Mum had a cut just above her eye, which was all swollen up. She said she'd banged it on one of the kitchen cupboard doors but she wouldn't look at me. Dad put his arm around her and gave her a big bear hug and said it was a shame that Old Clumsy Klutz couldn't go anywhere looking like that.

She rang the shop manager and said she was sorry but she wouldn't be coming. The next Saturday, when her eye was almost healed up, Dad took us all out for the day to a theme park. It was the best day ever. He was really nice to Mum and bought Grace and me birthstone bracelets, ice creams and cute soft toys even though I told him we were much too old for them. He bought Mum a beautiful necklace with metallic beads on a heavy chain which she said was lovely. She doesn't wear it often in case it gets broken.

I went on every single ride at least three times with Dad and I couldn't stop laughing when we went down the log flume, even though we got totally soaked. I even went on the death ride and felt so proud and happy when Dad told me I'd got some guts, and I giggled like mad when he joked that he'd just lost all his.

When we got home, everything was great, except we didn't see Auntie Anna any more, even though Mum promised she wouldn't ever try getting another job. Dad smiled and said, 'That's my girl,' and for some reason I thought everything was going to be all right from then on, but I was just a kid in those days and didn't know anything.

Mum's busy loading the suitcase and our sleeping bags into the boot when we go into the garage. My bag is really heavy and it's hard work trying to heave it onto the back seat before she can see. Grace spots it wriggling slightly, shoots me a glance and I know that she knows.

'He'd better keep quiet,' she whispers, helping me lower the bag carefully onto the floor, out of sight.

'He always sleeps in the car,' I whisper back, hoping and praying that tonight won't be any different.

'One of you in the front one in the back,' says Mum, gently closing the boot of the car. 'And no arguments, eh?'

Grace gives me another look and smiles as she climbs in the

front passenger seat. I get in the back, secretly reach my hand down into my bag and gently stroke the soft, warm, furry body inside.

Five minutes later, we're turning out of our driveway and heading up our road. It's raining now. In another hour's time, Dad will be home, expecting homemade steak and onion pie on the table. But there won't be any pie and there won't be any us. I start to giggle. I don't know why but I can't stop, even though I know it's not the slightest bit funny. I look back at our house as we drive around the corner and get a tight feeling in my chest. I can't help blurting out, 'What's Dad going to say?'

Mum is gripping the steering wheel tightly and doesn't take her eyes off the road.

'Don't worry, Ellie,' she says quietly. 'We'll be so far away we won't hear him.'

Chapter 6

Grace

Is this a dream? Or one of Ellie's fantasies? Any minute now Mum's going to spin the car around and say, 'OK, the adventure's over, we've gone far enough – better get home now.'

But she doesn't. We drive on and the rush hour traffic builds. I have to keep calm. Make a list or two.

OK.

Black cat (lucky).

Traffic Warden (grumpy).

Pizza delivery boy (spotty).

Men digging hole (mucky).

See. It works. Everything's going to be all right.

Man up telegraph pole (dodgy).

Woman in chicken costume handing out leaflets (weird).

Old lady with pram and —

Ellie's complaining that she's feeling carsick.

'I'll stop and you can swap with Grace and sit in the front,' Mum tells her, but she won't.

Mum stops anyway, we need petrol. As she fills up the

car, I wonder whether she's got the money to pay for it. It's only Thursday today and Dad doesn't give her anything until tomorrow.

I look out of the window and watch the petrol pump until the numbers on the dial finally grind to a halt. Mum catches my eye as she clicks the pump nozzle back into its slot. She's not wearing her usual dangly pearl earrings or the big gold locket that Gran gave her for her twenty-first birthday.

She disappears into the petrol station to pay and Ellie opens her canvas bag. A sleepy Bruno pokes his nose out, yawns and sniffs the air, deciding he can smell food. Suddenly he's wriggling out of the bag and scrabbling his way into the front of the car.

'Grace, do something!' Ellie orders, as if I can perform miracles. 'Stop him!'

But Mum's already coming back and Bruno's determined to get his face inside the carrier bag at my feet. I rescue the bag but it's too late to even think about hiding him again.

'Oh Grace!' says Mum as she gets back into the driver's seat. 'What on earth do you think you're doing?'

I look down and grip the plastic bag tighter. I can feel my lips clamping firmly together.

'Grace, talk to me!' Mum urges. 'Please.'

My eyes meet hers but I can't speak, I can't say a single word. The silence cuts me like a knife.

She looks away and shakes her head sadly.

'It wasn't her, it was me,' Ellie blurts out.

'But I told you we couldn't take him.'

'It'll be all right Mum. I'll look after him. Promise. I brought some tins of dog food and his bowl and lead. It's all here in my bag.'

Mum sits, staring out of the car window, biting her lip. She touches her throat where her locket chain should be, gives a little sigh and rubs the skin below her bruises, as if the locket might magically appear.

'Mum, please . . .' Ellie pleads.

As if he understands the situation, Bruno climbs from my lap onto Mum's and starts licking her face.

'Ow! Bruno, stop it!' she protests, but she's half smiling now, even though tears are rolling down her cheeks. Bruno's confused and licks harder, his nose wrinkling slightly at the salty taste on his tongue.

'OK. OK. Good boy, Bruno,' Mum says, finally unable to resist patting him. 'Ellie, I told you no, but he's with us now so he'll have to stay.'

She ushers him into the back of the car next to Ellie, who buries her face in his fur and hugs him like a long lost friend. We drive off, taking the motorway turning, heading west.

So why did Mum take off her locket and earrings? She never takes them off. Why would she pack them?

And then it hits me. I realise exactly what she's done; she's sold them to raise some money. And for the first time it really sinks in.

We're not going back.

Chapter 7

Ellie

As we drive down the motorway, Mum asks Grace to take out some of the sandwiches she's packed. They're cheese with homemade mango pickle, my favourite. The bread is fresh and crumbly and I suddenly realise I haven't eaten anything since lunchtime and I'm starving. I take a tiny but careful nibble out of the sandwich. I'm not feeling sick any more but I'm worried I might drop crumbs everywhere. Then I remember that Dad isn't going to inspect the car and see them, so I relax and tuck in.

'There's some cake too,' Mum says as I start on my second sandwich. Grace reaches into the bag again, and like a magician pulls out two slabs of Mum's delicious toffee and banana cake. As she hands me one, I can't help noticing the time on her watch.

Grace has seen it too. She stiffens and the colour slowly drains out of her face. She glances up at me then turns around and sits motionless, her piece of cake lying uneaten on her lap. And I know what's going through her mind because it's going through mine too. Dad is coming through the front door right this minute.

The house is always quiet and spotlessly tidy when he arrives home, so today won't be any different. He'll put down his briefcase and won't even notice we're not there – not at first. He'll shake out the creases then carefully hang up his coat in the hall cupboard before going into the kitchen. No Mum. He'll sniff. No steak and onion pie in the oven. Maybe he'll flick up the hem of the tablecloth and peer under the kitchen table. No Bruno. He'll be puzzled now. Suspicious even. He'll rub his beard with the tips of his fingers then go into the living room. There'll be no homework laid out on the table. No Grace. No Ellie. No Mum. He'll frown, then storm upstairs and check each room. No one. His eyes will be hard now and his lips clamped together in that grim expression he has when he's just about to lose it.

My heart beats faster. I glance at Grace. Three beads of sweat sit on her white forehead. She's breathing deeply and swallowing hard. She hasn't touched the cake on her lap.

'Mum . . . I think Grace is going to be sick.'

Mum turns and looks at her.

'Oh no, Grace . . . not now!' There's panic in Mum's voice. We're on the motorway. She can't pull over. 'Open the window. Get some fresh air . . . Grace, you're never car sick!' But Grace isn't listening. She grabs an empty carrier bag and throws up into it.

The smell is horrible but we have to drive on until we reach the next exit. Mum pulls off and stops the car as soon as she can. We all get out and stand on the grass verge. Mum tells Grace to take some deep breaths and gives her some water to drink while I let Bruno out of the car. He's excited after being cooped up for so long and thinks we've arrived but he runs straight into the road.

'Bruno!' I yell as I chase after him. A dark grey car comes round the corner, heading straight towards me. My heart misses a beat.

Remember, I'll always find you out, Ellie. Always. If you tell tales – you won't get away with it. Ever. Dad's threat from last night rings in my ears.

Mum's yelling at me to get out of the road but I don't move. I can't. It's him. He's come to get us. He slams on the brakes and screeches to a halt inches away from me.

'Ellie!' Mum shouts. She grabs hold of my arm and Bruno's collar and drags us back to the side of the road. 'What are you doing?'

'It's Dad!' I tell her, too frightened to look.

I can hear him opening the window and shouting at me. But his voice is different, high pitched and not at all like it normally is. When I finally pluck up courage and look, I realise it's not Dad after all. It's not even a man with a beard; it's a woman with short grey hair. I start giggling again. In fact, it's so funny I just can't stop laughing. I suck in big mouthfuls of air and it feels good to let out the weird shrieking noise from deep inside me, even though it makes the woman who isn't Dad crosser.

'I'm sorry!' Mum calls to her as Grace takes Bruno. 'Sorry. Our dog ran off and . . .'

The woman shakes her head, mutters something and drives away, and now Mum's holding my arms, telling me to stop, calm down – I could have been run over, why on earth did I just stand there – but all I can think about is that it's not Dad. It's not him. He hasn't found us. Gradually the giggles subside and I'm left with a tired, empty feeling and a bad stitch, like I've been running for too long.

Mum hugs me, then we get into the car and drive back onto the motorway. It goes on forever and ever and there's nothing to look at but the tail- or headlights of other cars and lorries. She turns on the radio but no one's listening so she flicks it off and we drive on in silence. Grace closes her eyes but I think she's just pretending to be asleep. There are fewer cars now and it's getting late.

'Try to sleep if you can,' Mum whispers over her shoulder to me.

'Where are we going?' I ask.

She doesn't reply.

'Mum? We can't just drive for ever.'

'We won't. Go to sleep. I'll wake you when we're there.'

It's dark outside, my eyes feel heavy, and although I know I won't be able to sleep, it gets harder and harder to keep them open. Bruno snuggles closer to me and gives a yawn.

Chapter 8

Grace

The last thing I expect to see when I wake up is a sparkling green-blue sea but here it is, shimmering magically away right in front of me, picture postcard beautiful but frighteningly close. The water's choppy, and waves with frothy peaks break onto the sandy beach below us and crash onto rocks out to sea. The sun's shining but the wind's strong and from time to time it shakes our car with powerful gusts as it blows cotton wool clouds across the sky. We're the only car in the car park – and it seems as if we've driven to the edge of the world and stopped, just in time.

I glance at Mum fast asleep next to me, with her cheek resting on her hand and a faint frown creasing the delicate skin between her eyebrows. The bruise on her neck looks painful and sore. My unzipped sleeping bag is spread over us but it's slipping off her, so I gently lift it and carefully lay it back over her again. She stirs like a little child, gives a gentle groan, but doesn't wake.

On the back seat, Ellie's curled up with Bruno, both snuggled under her sleeping bag, just the tops of their heads showing. Bruno's making the funny little growly noises he often makes in his sleep, and judging by the twitching of his nose, is probably dreaming about chasing rabbits. It's seven a.m. and there's no one around. A flock of seagulls swoops overhead, filling the air with their deafening squawking. Bruno wakes up and barks excitedly, which instantly wakes Mum and Ellie.

'Are we here?' asks Ellie, sitting up sleepily. She peers out of the car window, her mouth open in disbelief. 'Oh my . . .' Her voice trails off and she stares at the shimmering sea as if it's a mirage.

'I came here on holiday once, when I was ten,' says Mum quietly. 'With Anna, Gran and Grandad, the year before he died. I expect it's all different now.'

We sit staring out through the windscreen at the sea below.

'Hey! What's that?' shouts Ellie suddenly. She's pointing at three shiny dark grey footballs bobbing up and down in the water. Puzzled, we peer down, realizing the footballs have eyes, snouts and whiskers.

'Seals!' Mum says excitedly. 'They're seals!'

I've only ever seen seals before on TV and just once at the theme park Dad took us to, after he hit Mum that first time. She knew I hated all the screamy rides and I've got a thing about heights – standing on a chair is an adventure – but Dad was getting twitchy because it had cost a packet to get in and now I didn't want to go on anything, so she suggested we all looked at the animals for a bit. Seeing them cooped up in their tiny pens and cages was even more depressing so Dad and Ellie went back on the rides again.

Mum and I went and sat down by the white concrete pool and watched as the keeper tried to bribe some seals with lumps of smelly fish in return for pushing a doorbell and clapping their flippers together and other essential marine life-skills. But the seals weren't interested and completely lost the plot when the fish ran out. They lay down right where they were, and went on strike, which secretly made me want to cheer.

At the end of the show I glanced over at Mum to see if she wanted to go. She was sitting perfectly still next to me, but behind her dark sunglasses I saw tears rolling down her cheeks, even though her lips were bent up into a smile. I reached for her hand and held it tight and we sat through the show all over again, until Dad came to find us with Ellie.

The seals swimming here look totally different. They're bursting with energy. We watch them for ages as they play around the rocks before finally swimming out to sea and disappearing.

'Grandad used to tease me that seals were really mermaids in disguise,' Mum tells us. 'He told us a story about their tears turning into priceless pearls. And we believed it. We used to get up early, Anna and I, and hunt through the seaweed on the beach for them.'

'I bet these are the grandchildren of the ones you saw,' says Ellie.

She's desperate to get out and explore but Mum makes her clip Bruno's lead onto his collar before we open the car doors. It feels good to be out in the fresh salty air after being stuck inside the car for so long. We give Bruno some water poured into the old dog bowl Ellie's brought, then set off along the path. The wind blows our hair across our faces and we look like wild things but none of us care. Bruno is excited too and pulls on his lead, wanting to explore every dip and hollow in the short springy grass in case it's the start of a rabbit burrow. We wind our way down the path to the beach, take off our shoes and walk barefoot along the damp sand.

There are a few people around now, walking their dogs or fishing. We're heading for the little rickety wooden shack on stilts at the far end of the beach.

'It used to be a café,' Mum tells us.

'Hope it still is – I'm starving,' Ellie says.

It is still a café but it's closed. Disappointed, we sit on its weather-beaten wooden steps wondering what to do next when an old man with a fierce expression and a shock of white hair appears behind the window and stares down at us. We all jump and Ellie gives a little squeal.

He unlocks the door and pokes his head outside.

'Not open till eight!' he snaps. Ellie pulls a face, which he notices. 'Was it breakfast you're wanting or just drinks?'

'Um, breakfast, please,' Mum tells him.

He waves to one of the fishermen carrying a bucket and rod, making his way towards the hut. 'Well, come on then,' he announces gruffly. 'Might as well do yours and Bill's together.'

Despite his scary-looking appearance, we don't need asking twice. Mum takes Bruno's lead and is about to tie him up when the man tuts.

'Aw, bring him in. Don't stand on ceremony here!'

Chapter 9

Ellie

The old man tells us he's seventy-one and has a gammy knee that gives him jip, whatever that is, on cold damp days like this. He says it in a voice that makes it sound like it's our fault, but Mum replies that she knows how miserable arthritis is, because her mum had it. This calms him down a bit and he tells us his name is Stan, he's too old for this cooking lark, but to sit ourselves down.

There are six tables squashed into the room with three or four chairs tucked around each one. None of the chairs match but I decide I like this because you can choose the one that fits your size or your mood. We sit down at a round table covered with a red and white checked tablecloth and I can't help noticing there's a huge rip in the middle and the flowers in the vase died last century. Dad would have complained and walked straight out but Mum doesn't even seem to notice.

Stacked against the walls of the café are all sorts of bits and pieces: metal buckets, fishing nets and rods, some giant pinky-white shells and even an old rusty anchor propped against the wooden panelling in the corner next to a battered piano. Jammed between a tower of lobster pots and what looks like a torture machine (but Mum tells me is just an old fashioned mangle used for squeezing water out of wet washing), is a bookshelf crammed full of books about tropical fish, a collection of dusty, prickly cactus plants and an empty goldfish bowl. Maybe Stan hates running the café because he really wants to run a junk shop instead.

As he fries up sausages, bacon, eggs and tomatoes in the biggest frying pan I've ever seen, he tells us how he and his wife, Daphne, own the café and a nearby caravan site, and asks where we're staying.

'We're not sure yet,' Mum replies, nervously adjusting her scarf, so it covers her bruised neck completely. 'We've only just arrived.'

'Got some vans empty till the season starts. How long you thinking of staying?'

Mum looks flustered. I can see she doesn't know what to say, but Stan doesn't seem to notice and waits for a reply.

'Um . . . a few weeks . . . maybe longer.'

A flicker of surprise crosses Stan's wrinkled brown face but then he nods.

'We came away in a bit of a rush,' I chip in. 'Mum thought, wouldn't it be nice to have a bit of a holiday, and we said, yeah, great . . . bring it on, let's stay by the sea . . . so here we are.' I give a strange little laugh. Grace is glaring at me to shut up but I can't, I keep on babbling. 'It's really lovely here, isn't it? We saw seals just now. Some people think they're mermaids and their tears can change into pearls. That would be great, wouldn't it? You'd just have to find them, collect them in a bucket or something and then you'd be rich. You could do whatever you liked. No more worries. Ever . . .'

I stop, finally running out of steam.

'Hear that, Billy Boy?' says Stan with a laugh to the old fisherman sitting in the corner. 'I told you you're wasting your time with fish.'

'Huh. Never catch them, neither,' Bill retorts gloomily as Stan dishes up our breakfasts and brings them over.

We thank him politely as he puts down the plates in front of us, and I tuck in eagerly.

'Not hungry then?' Stan jokes as he hovers at the table, watching us eat, which makes Grace nervous, but doesn't bother me. Mum tells him it's delicious and thanks him again, even though her bacon's burnt and all our egg yokes are mangled to bits. A few seconds later, he seems to have made up his mind about something.

'I can rent you a caravan for a good price. It's quite small and not the best on the site, but it's clean and got everything you'll need. You can have it on a weekly basis. Stay as long as you want.'

'Thank you,' says Mum looking relieved. 'Thank you very much. That would be . . . ideal.'

Stan nods, then goes back behind the counter as a couple of windswept hikers come in for breakfast.

When we've finished, Mum pays and Stan gets his walking stick. He leaves Bill in charge of the café and we set off along the sandy path through the dunes until it opens up into a large field edged with trees and bushes. Rows of caravans, some huge, some tiny, some with their own little gardens and fences, are spaced out on the grass. We head for a windowless shed at the road entrance to the site which Stan calls his office. He unlocks it and we wait outside while he finds the key to our caravan.

'I'll only need a small deposit,' he tells Mum as he gives her a key ring with several keys attached.

Mum looks worried and mumbles an excuse about having to get to the bank. Confused because she doesn't have a bank account, I glance at Grace, who gives me another 'shut up' glare.

'No rush,' Stan says as he locks the door of the shed behind him.

'Thank you,' says Mum.

'Number twenty-one.' He points to the far end of the site. 'It's right in front of the path to the stones.'

'Stones?' I ask.

'You won't miss them Maids. Just see if you can count 'em all.'

I look at him puzzled but he doesn't explain.

'Better get back,' he says, 'Bill's not exactly your Jamie Oliver. Tried to fry the baked beans last time I left him in charge.'

With that he limps back along the path towards the café.

We head over to the other side of the site and start looking for number twenty-one. We pass a lady with short blond hair and thick dark-rimmed glasses sitting on the step of her caravan, muffled up in a red coat. She's busy typing on the laptop perched on her knees but she looks up, smiles and gives us a little wave as we pass.

Dad says caravans are common, but I've always secretly wanted to stay in one. I love the idea of living in your own miniature house on wheels. I go hot and cold as I suddenly wonder what he's doing right now. He should be on his way to work – but would he go as normal or would he try and find us? Could he find us? I'm sure Mum wouldn't have said anything to him about where we were going but he's always had this horrible way of worming things out of you that you don't want him to know. I peer back at the site entrance, half expecting him to drive through it at any moment.

'Ellie!' Mum calls. 'Number twenty-one! We've found it!'

I turn around to see her and Grace standing by a tatty pale green caravan with a gently rounded roof, surrounded by brambles and wedged into the corner of the site, next to a path. Unafraid of getting prickled, Bruno's sniffing around the bottom edge of the caravan, his tail wagging madly. I double check the site entrance and tell myself to stop worrying, then run over to Mum and Grace as Mum finds the right key and unlocks the door to our new home.

Chapter 10

Grace

'Eurgh! Smells like something's died in here!' says Ellie, wrinkling her nose as we step inside.

'Don't exaggerate, love,' Mum tells her. 'It just hasn't been used for a while.' She goes to a window and tries to open it but it's locked so she sorts through the keys and finds the right one. 'It'll be fine.'

She looks worried as she pushes the window open, but I'm pretty sure it's got nothing to do with the musty pong in here; she's wondering how on earth she's going to pay Stan. I check my dress pocket and pull out my little embroidered purse. I can't remember if there's any money in here or not. I unzip it and discover a scrap of paper with a list of all my favourite dress designers and a folded up twenty pound note which Dad gave me a couple of weeks ago for passing my last violin exam. I hand the money to Mum and she hugs me.

'Thanks, sweetheart,' she whispers.

'I haven't got anything,' Ellie says, giving me a scowl then eyeing Mum anxiously.

'Don't worry, darling. We'll manage somehow,' she says.

'Cheer up, let's make ourselves at home.'

So we do. There's:

One little bedroom with bunk beds (for Ellie and me).

One tiny bathroom (smaller than my wardrobe back home).

One living space (with two cushioned bench seats and table that will convert into a bed for Mum).

One narrow galley kitchen (with four cupboards, a tiny sink, a fridge and a cooker).

And that's it.

Mum goes off to get the car and when she comes back we unload our stuff and spend the next couple of hours sweeping and wiping and cleaning everything until the caravan looks and smells fresh and clean. Mum goes outside and starts to cut away the brambles growing up by the door while Ellie and I stow away our things into the little lockers in our tiny bedroom. I'm about to put my violin case up on the shelf with my sewing stuff when I suddenly feel a sharp pang of guilt because I'm supposed to practise every day for at least an hour.

Hesitantly, I take out my violin and play a few notes but can't remember the piece I've been learning and haven't brought any music with me. As it dawns on me that it doesn't matter any more, my frustration melts away. I junk the exam piece and begin to improvise on my favourite song from the charts. As I play louder and more confidently, Ellie closes her eyes and starts swaying her arms over her head as if she were at a pop festival or something.

'It's like being on holiday,' she says.

But it isn't. Ever since I can remember, holidays with Dad were horrible. We were always on our best behaviour, walking on eggshells so he didn't have anything to get angry about. We could never let our hair down and be silly, or make a noise like this. He would have gone ballistic. But now we're dancing on eggshells.

Mum peeps round the doorway. She's holding some delicate pink flowers.

'Sweet briar,' she tells us. 'Only flowers once a year. Found it under the brambles.' She's taken off her coat and scarf and although the bruise on her neck looks darker than yesterday, she laughs as she joins in, dancing with Ellie. Bruno bounds in next, determined not to miss out on the fun, but the room's far too tiny for three people and a dog to jump around in without knocking each other unconscious, so after less than a minute, Mum and Ellie flop down on the bottom bunk bed to catch their breath and Bruno leaps on top of them and starts licking them to death.

I finish the tune with a flourish and Mum and Ellie clap, so I give a little bow before putting my violin back in its case.

'I've never heard you play like that before!' says Ellie astonished.

No one's ever heard me play like that before.

I loved learning my violin until Dad realised I was actually quite good at it, because then the pressure started. I had to practise every piece over and over to score top marks in each grade, even though my head often felt like it was going to explode. I quickly learnt to hide anything else I was good at, just like Mum hides her cuts and bruises.

I reach up to the shelf to put my violin away and notice the brown paper bag. I hand it to Mum who looks inside, then gives a gasp.

'Oh Grace, I don't believe it! You saved it!'

She holds the folded quilt gently in her hands and smells it, as if the faint scent of Gran's fingers as she sewed it might still be traced, then we go into the main room where she spreads it out carefully over the bench seat.

She stares at it as if she can't take it all in at once. 'So many memories,' she whispers, with a slight shake of her head, 'all sewn in here together.'

As she runs her fingers over the different patches of fabric, her face slowly crumples and she looks as if she's going to cry.

'Don't be sad, Mum,' says Ellie. 'Gran would be really happy if she knew you'd still got it.'

'I know,' Mum says nodding, as her fingers move onto the yellow and white daisies and her face lights up with a smile.

'What?' asks Ellie.

'My best summer dress when I was a kid. Gran made it. It had a plain white collar and pockets and I wore it for the first time when I took my exam for grammar school.'

'I didn't know you went to a grammar school!' says Ellie, impressed.

'I nearly didn't. The day of the entrance exam, Grandad's car wouldn't start. We lived in a village and there were no buses, but he was determined I was going to take that exam so we started walking, even though we both knew we were going to be too late. A mile down the lane, a tractor was about to pass us but Grandad flagged it down and persuaded the farmer to make a diversion. So I certainly made an entrance. When I opened the cab door, two sheep jumped down with me. Most of the other girls turned up in posh cars with their parents.'

She gives a little giggle and suddenly I can see her, ten years old, her hair in pigtails wearing that little dress with yellow daisies. 'I'll never forget the way they turned and looked at me, their noses all wrinkled.'

'But you passed . . .'

Mum nods shyly. 'They gave me a scholarship too, money for books and equipment and stuff.'

'You must have been really clever.'

Mum shrugs her thin shoulders. 'Maybe . . .' She hangs her head. 'Not any more though.'

I suddenly remember what our Dad used to call her. 'You stupid cow,' he'd say, and worse. 'You're as thick as two short planks.'

Chapter 11

Ellie

We feed Bruno and fold the rug from the boot of the car to make him a bed, then Grace and I explore, taking the path behind our caravan through the woods. We soon come to a clearing surrounded by trees. There's no one here and it's dead quiet. Spaced around the clearing is a circle of old weather-worn stones, some as tall and thin as us, others smaller or fatter or just stumps, half buried under the grass.

We start to count them.

'Fifteen,' says Grace firmly.

'No, sixteen. Did you count that little one poking out by that bush?' I ask, convinced I'm right.

We both count once more. This time she makes it sixteen but I can only find fifteen even though I definitely counted the little one.

'Wonder why Stan calls them Maids?' Grace asks. 'They don't look like maids or even people at all.'

'He's obviously bonkers,' I say with a shrug. 'Let's face it, his café's pretty weird with all that junk.' Another idea pops into my head. 'Or maybe . . . it's his wife who's doolally and he calls them Maids because that's what she thinks they are. And it's all her stuff in the café, and she keeps collecting more and more and he's got to stop her but she won't listen, and they're drowning in junk, so he ends up locking her up at home, like Mr Rochester's wife in *Jane Eyre* . . . except they're both older and a lot more wrinkly and they don't have an attic, just a dormer bungalow with a little bedroom upstairs . . .'

As usual, Grace isn't listening. She's gently touching the tallest stone, tracing its rough surface with her fingers. She gives a shiver.

'What's going to happen, Ellie?' she asks suddenly.

'What d'you mean? Is she going to creep out one night and torch the café or something?'

'No! To us. Mum, you and me.'

I think for a moment before I reply. Why should only stories have happy endings? It's not fair. I want one too. 'We're going to start a brand new life and it's going to be fan-flipping-tastic.' I tell her. 'Grace, no one knows us here. We can be anyone we want now.'

'But what about Dad? What if he finds us?'

I don't want to think about this. 'How could he?' I reply nervously. 'He doesn't even know where we are.'

Grace pulls a face but doesn't say anything. Suddenly neither of us feels like exploring any more so we head back to the caravan, passing the lady in the red coat. She's carrying a notebook and a camera but she doesn't look like she's on holiday – more like she's working.

'Settled in OK?' she asks, smiling at us.

'Yes thanks,' I say, trying not to look at her suspiciously.

'By the way, tell your mum she's an amazing violinist —'

'Oh, that was Grace,' I blurt out without thinking.

The woman turns to her and says, 'You're very talented. How long have you been learning?'

Grace stares at her nervously and doesn't reply. There's an

awkward silence. I have to say something or else we'll both look weird. If she's a private detective or something, hired by Dad, I've already pooped it.

'About four years,' I say warily.

The lady looks bemused but then smiles at us both.

'Well, it was wonderful to hear you play. It helped me think – cleared my mind. I was totally stuck on my next chapter and after you'd finished I suddenly knew exactly what to write.'

'You're a writer?' I say, surprised. 'You don't look like one.'

'Sorry . . . So, what do writers look like?'

'Don't know. Never met one before.' I don't tell her she looks much too ordinary. Scruffy even. I also don't tell her that I wanted to be a writer once – but a glamorous, rich one, in clicky heels and smart clothes, not a bit like her.

'I'm researching my next book – making notes and planning everything out at the moment.'

'What's it about?' I ask.

'Myths and legends from around the country.'

'Any vampires in it?'

'Um, not so far . . .' She clocks my disappointment. 'But plenty of other gory stuff though. Stan's been a great help. Knows all the folklore around here.'

'He told us to try and count the stones.'

'And me. In fact, I've counted them every day, and never made the same number twice in a row . . . Hopeless!'

'We did too.'

'Well, that's the beauty of the Maids, apparently – just when you think you've got them pegged, something happens and the story changes. I've been here two weeks and I'm still not sure what to make of them – except a couple are definitely a little loose in the ground.'

'I bet someone's moving them around,' I say. 'In the dead of night.'

'Maybe,' she replies with a laugh. 'I'm sure a touch of

mystery's good for the tourist trade. I noticed they're selling glow-in-the-dark stone circles down in the gift shop, yesterday.'

'But why are they called Maids?' I ask.

'The main legend, and there are loads, says they were young girls, turned to stone by a thunderbolt. Bit harsh though, don't you think, just for dancing on a Sunday?' She shakes her head and smiles. 'Well, better get some work done. I'm Susan by the way. Susan Grey.' She turns to Grace. 'I'll be listening out, so feel free to play that fiddle whenever you like. And you never know, maybe you'll wake them up and they'll start dancing again,' she adds with a nod to the stones.

Grace smiles politely and we carry on down the path until we reach the caravan field. Thoughts of Dad creep back into my head so I try to distract myself by imagining people I've never met — dancing maids, Stan's mad wife . . . and my grandad hijacking that tractor to get Mum to her exam on time. If only he was still alive now, I think, he could help us. I give a little sigh. He isn't here. We're on our own so we've just got to help ourselves.

Suddenly, a half-formed idea starts to whirl around my head. On impulse, I tell Grace that I'm just popping back to the beach for a few minutes and then run off before she can tell me not to. I reach the café and peep inside. It's lunchtime now and busy. Plucking up courage, I push open the door.

'You again?' says Stan abruptly, dumping down plates of sausage and chips in front of two customers and then hurrying back to get two more.

'Excuse me,' a woman calls from a nearby table, 'We ordered some pasties —'

'Won't be a moment,' Stan replies. He looks flustered now. 'Can't chat,' he snaps as he passes me. 'If I don't get four pasties and a bowl of chips on that table, there's going to be mayhem.'

'You need some help,' I say, seizing the moment and following him back to the counter. He takes out the pasties from the fridge.

'Chance would be a fine thing.'

'Mum's looking for a job.'

'Thought you were on holiday?' He hurriedly drops some uncooked chips into a pan full of bubbling hot fat.

'Well . . . We are . . . but . . .'

Stan stops what he's doing and looks me in the eye, which is pretty scary, but I don't flinch, even though I'm wondering whether trying to get Mum a job here is actually the most sensible idea in the world considering how grumpy he is, let alone the fact he has a mad wife locked away.

'It's sort of complicated,' I tell him, taking the plunge, 'but she's a great cook and you need some help so why don't you give her a try?'

'So what does she say about this grand plan of yours?' asks Stan.

'She'd jump at it,' I lie. 'In fact, she was just saying last week how she'd love to run a café like this . . .'

Years of hiding stuff about home and Dad have made me a pretty convincing liar. I'm not proud of it but it's about the only thing I'm good at.

Three more customers come in and sit down at a table that needs clearing. They look at the dirty crockery and one of them mumbles something about going somewhere else.

'Be with you in a tick,' Stan calls to them.

'You could spend more time with Daphne if Mum was here,' I add, carefully watching his reaction.

He pulls a face then says gruffly, 'OK. Tell your mum to pop up here at five. We'll talk then.'

'It's a deal.'

'I'm not promising anything, mind.'

'I know. Thanks. Bye then . . .'

He nods, then hurriedly serves up the pasties and chips as I whizz towards the door.

'Oh . . . we counted the stones . . .' I tell him.

'And?'

'Fifteen?'

Stan gives a short laugh.

'Sixteen?' I say.

He shakes his head. 'Pah!' he tuts.

Chapter 12

Grace

When Ellie tells me her plan, I give her a whole list of reasons why it's a bad idea, but as usual, she goes all out, determined to convince Mum.

'It's totally perfect!' she protests. 'You help in the café and Stan lets us live in the caravan for free. What could be better?'

'Life doesn't work like that Ellie,' Mum tells her with a frown as she wipes the little bathroom window with a damp cloth. 'It's far too simple. Besides I don't know the first thing about running a café. What if I mess up or burn the place down? Let's face it: I'd be useless.'

That's what Dad used to say all the time. 'You're useless, Karin,' he'd insist, whether she was doing her hair or making a cup of tea. 'Utterly useless. A complete waste of space.' She could never do anything right. He's drummed this into her so many times I think she believes it now.

'Course you won't be useless,' Ellie insists.

Mum shakes her head but Ellie doesn't give up.

'Stan wants to spend more time with Daphne. You'll be helping him out.'

A little later we sit down at the tiny table in the caravan, and eat the last of the sandwiches. They're soggy and sad but apart from a bit of Mum's cake, some cereal and a few tins of soup, it's all the food we've got left. Mum says she's doesn't want any and cuts the cake into two pieces.

'Why don't we just go and see Stan?' Ellie asks. 'Then you can talk it over with him.'

'I suppose I'll have to face him sooner or later to tell him we only have the money to pay for a few more nights, so I might as well get it over and done with,' she says. 'But I'm not working in that café . . . so just stop going on about it. Please.'

I don't say 'I told you so' to Ellie because I know she's only trying to help. And the thing is, now I've had time to think about it, Ellie's right for once; it would be the perfect job for Mum. She's spent years at home cooking and cleaning and waiting on Dad, making sure everything was exactly right so he didn't have any reason to get cross with her. Not that it helped. He still lost his temper all the time. Behind his back, Mum used to make excuses for him – like he worked too hard – but even as a kid I didn't believe her, especially when she'd blame herself. Sometimes I wonder if he got angry because she did everything so beautifully. He liked it much better when he had to come to her rescue or he could put her right on something or just let rip and have a go at her.

The more I think about it, the more I want Mum to have this job. I don't eat my piece of cake but wrap it carefully in a paper serviette and tuck it in my pocket when no one's looking. At five to five we leave Bruno in the caravan, lock the door and walk along the path through the dunes to the café on the beach.

There are no customers now and Stan's busy washing up.

'Shall I put the kettle on?' Ellie asks as we step through the door. I throw her a look but she chucks it back at me.

'Make yourself at home,' says Stan, glaring at her from under his fierce bushy eyebrows, but his sarcasm is wasted as

Ellie makes a beeline for the kettle.

Nervously, Mum starts to explain that we won't be staying in the caravan for long after all.

'So you don't want a job now?' asks Stan impatiently.

'We . . . um . . . we're not sure we can afford —'

'So a job would come in handy then?'

'Well – yes, but —'

'You worked in a café before?'

'No.'

'Cooking and hygiene qualifications?'

'No.'

'Any references then – from a previous employer?'

Mum doesn't even bother answering. She stares down uncomfortably at the floor, the same way she used to when Dad lectured her on her cooking or told her what a bad parent she was, not like his mum and dad.

Stan shakes his head. 'I've got enough problems on my plate. Bill can't tell the difference between a courgette and a baguette, but he's my brother and at least I can rely on him.'

Mum looks embarrassed and starts to get up. 'I'm sorry. We'd better go —'

'You can't. Tea's ready,' says Ellie, quickly putting two mugs in front of Stan and Mum.

'Have this first,' says Stan gruffly, 'and don't mind me. It's not personal.'

Reluctantly, she sits down again. I quickly unwrap the piece of cake from my jacket pocket and place it carefully on a clean plate. It's a little squashed but I carry it over to Stan and place it on the table in front of him. Ellie catches on and looks at me hopefully.

'Mum made this,' she tells Stan. 'Banana and toffee, but she can make all sorts, and pies and pasties and anything really. She's the most fantastic cook in the world —'

'Ellie, don't tell tales —'

44

'Well, you are! You just don't know it.'

Stan shakes his head, looking at each of us in turn before picking up the piece of cake, inspecting it carefully then taking a large bite. We watch him as he slowly chews then swallows. He takes another bite, then another, and another, until the last crumb is gone. Then he sits quietly for a moment.

'We open at eight for cooked breakfasts until twelve then we do lunches. We serve morning coffees and afternoon teas. We shut at five – nine on Saturdays,' he says finally.

Mum nods politely, glancing at the door, wanting to go.

'So I'll see you at ten to eight tomorrow then.'

'I've got the job?' asks Mum, surprised.

'I'd be an idiot if I didn't take you on. Even Daphne didn't used to cook as good as this.'

Ellie turns round and lets out a silent 'Yes!' and I can't help grinning.

'I told you!' she says jubilantly.

Stan shows Mum round the kitchen and explains if she works four days every week, her wages will cover the rent for the caravan and there'll be money over.

'You'll have to make some homemade cakes and pasties, though,' he orders. 'Daphne used to handle all that but I'm buying in stuff now and it's not always very good.'

'Right,' says Mum, still looking stunned. 'Ten to eight tomorrow then.'

Chapter 13

Ellie

'Do I look OK?' asks Mum, nervously smoothing the creases in her white blouse. She's carefully wound a silk scarf around her neck and tied the ends in a little bow so her bruise can't be seen.

'Perfect,' I tell her, although to be honest there are dark shadows under her eyes and she looks as if she hasn't slept for a month. While she's working at the café today, we're going to walk into town, about half a mile away. She holds out Grace's twenty-pound note and a shopping list and tells us to hunt around for the cheapest prices. Grace nods at me as she takes the list, so I put the money carefully in my jacket pocket and zip it up.

'Good luck,' I say as Mum goes. 'Not that you'll need it,' I add quickly. She gives a nervous smile and waves as she hurries across the field towards the beach path.

Half an hour later, Grace, Bruno and I set off. We follow the road from the site entrance down into the town. The place is busy because there's a big market set up in the car park by the harbour. At the very end there's a stall selling handmade earrings and Grace spends ages looking at them all. I'm bored to bits so I wander back through the crowd, past the other stalls until I come to one crammed with hair accessories, brushes, combs and even a few packets of hair dye. I pick up one, looking at the picture on the front. The pretty-looking girl is smiling and her long bouncy hair is a glamorous bright blond, exactly how I've always wanted mine to be.

'Just two fifty today' says the man behind the stall.

I glance around and see Grace with her back to me, still looking at the jewellery. About two months ago some woman stopped us as we were coming out of a clothes shop and asked Grace if she'd ever thought of being a model, said she was a talent scout for some big agency. Course Grace didn't reply but when I said I'd definitely be interested, the woman just shook her head, smiled and said I wasn't quite what they were looking for. Flipping cheek.

I look at the packet again. Seeing me hesitate, the man winks.

'A pound for you, darling – you'd look amazing with hair that colour.'

Spending just one pound isn't going to hurt, I convince myself. Not to look amazing. And everything in the market is so cheap we'll have plenty of money for the food Mum wants us to buy.

'OK,' I say, unzipping my purse and offering the man Grace's twenty-pound note. Suddenly, I spot her heading my way so I hurriedly take the change, stuff it in a pocket then tuck the packet of hair dye under my jacket so she won't see it.

I wing my way back through the crowd to meet her, then we head over to the fruit and veg stall. We get everything Mum's put on the list and Grace adds it up as we go.

'Eleven pounds thirty-five,' she whispers to me but then as I reach into my pocket to pay, I realise to my horror that I've only got four pound coins. Both the ten and five pound notes have vanished.

'They must have fallen out,' I tell Grace, desperately.

Grace looks at me confused, and feeling guilty, I explain that I've spent a pound and lost most of the change. We have to give back half the stuff, annoying the stallholder, who curses at us under his breath. We retrace my steps to try and find the missing money but there's no sign of it.

Grace won't speak to me all the way home, even when one of the thin plastic bags holding the loose potatoes splits. They roll into the road and a couple of cars drive past, squashing some of them to pulp. When the coast is clear, I hold onto Bruno while she scrabbles about, rescuing what she can.

'I didn't mean to lose all that money,' I say miserably, as we step into the caravan a few minutes later.

She still doesn't reply, but heads into our little bedroom.

'I said I'm sorry!' I say, following her in. 'You don't have to blank me out too,' I add, getting cross now at her silence, 'cos let's face it, if you stop talking to me you might as well super-glue your lips together, like this.' I purse my lips together making a silly fish face but she doesn't react. 'And then one day when you do want to say something, and you unstick them, you won't remember how to talk any more. You'll open your mouth and a load of gobbledy-gook will fly out.'

Grace turns around, her blue eyes blazing. 'We're not living in one of your make-believe worlds, Ellie. We need that money.'

'I know! And I told you, I didn't lose it on purpose. Anyway, if you're so worried, why didn't you look after it in the first place? It was yours!'

I know full well why she didn't want it – so she wouldn't have to speak to anyone if we bought something.

'You won't even talk to Mum!' I say. 'How do you think she feels? She never says anything, but you really upset her.'

This is below the belt and I know it, but my big mouth just won't shut up. Her face crumples.

'I don't mean to,' she whispers.

'It's not like she's done anything.'

Grace doesn't reply but turns away from me.

'I don't understand you. You're so weird!' I tell her as I stomp out of the bedroom.

A few seconds later she comes out holding her canvas bag. She avoids my eye as she heads for the door.

'So what am I going to say to Mum about the money?' I ask.

'You'll think of some fairy story,' she mutters as she steps out of the caravan.

'Where are you going?'

'Nowhere.'

With that she slams the door behind her. I know she's angry too but I don't care. It's all right for her; everyone thinks she's amazing even when she doesn't say a word. Dad used to tell me off all the time, just for talking. *Do shut up, Ellie. You're such a drama queen. Why can't you be quiet like your sister?* he'd say in a disappointed voice.

Sitting down at the little table, I take out the packet of hair dye and unfold the instructions. There are a few diagrams but the words are in a foreign language that I don't recognise. I look at the girl on the packet again, beaming at me. 'How hard can it be?' I ask Bruno, heading for the little bathroom with my towel.

Chapter 14

Grace

I calm down a bit as I walk back to town. I want to explain things to Ellie but everything's so complicated – all tangled up. I don't know how or where to begin. I'm so different to her – she always sees life as black or white and if she doesn't like something she'll just make up some fantasy instead.

When she was seven, she decided she'd been abandoned by fairies and adopted by Mum and Dad. She called herself Araminta and wrote long sagas of her previous life, involving an evil wizard and a toad with a wooden leg called Neville (toad not leg), filling up notebook after notebook. *Imaginative* was the word her teachers used. Mum loved the spell ingredients (green custard and whelks mainly) and I had a soft spot for Neville, whose only mission in life was to hop out from under his stone and using his stump, trip up the wizard, causing him to fall head first into his cauldron, saving Araminta from his latest deadly concoction.

Unfortunately Dad wasn't impressed with any of it. He took the mickey out of Ellie's tales mercilessly until finally she stopped writing them. She told me she'd run out of ideas, but for Ellie to run out of ideas is like the sky running out of stars. A few weeks later she killed off Araminta for good by chucking every single notebook into the dustbin. The only stories she wrote after that were school essays, but for at least a year she carried on telling people she was adopted.

It's mid-morning now and the market is more packed than earlier. My hands are already shaking as I carefully choose my spot and run through the list in my head.

Stay calm.

Open bag.

Open violin case.

Pick up violin.

Deep deep breath.

Play.

Keep playing.

Somehow I do all this. A few people turn and stare, surprised at the sound of music, but I manage to carry on. Playing solo in last year's Christmas concert was a breeze compared to this.

I finish the tune and bow my head slightly. No one claps and from the corner of my eye, I see people just turn away or carry on walking. Embarrassed and disappointed, I'm wondering what to do next when a small child drops a fifty pence coin into my case. I look up as she runs back to her mum who's smiling at me and I give them both a grateful wave and start to play again – pop songs, folk ballads, anything I can think of that people might like to hear.

As I get into my stride, several people stop and listen and more coins are tossed into my case. An hour later, I can hardly see its red silk lining.

The music works its magic on me too. I hate people staring at me, but I manage to relax, because my violin is a kind of buffer between us. I'm safe in my own world while I play, because no one can try and make me talk to them.

Gradually I'm aware of a tall boy about my age, tanned with scruffy blond hair, standing nearby. Although it's cold he's wearing board shorts and an oversized bright blue T-shirt. As I glance at him, he tosses a pound coin into my violin case and grins. I nod and smile back, just as I've smiled at everyone else who's given me money, but there's something about him that throws me off my stride.

I play for another half hour and people come and go, but the boy doesn't budge. I'm tired and my fingers are getting sore, so I wind up the tune I'm playing. People clap, then realise I've stopped for good and everyone starts to disperse . . . except this boy. Unnerved, I bend down to collect up the money, but out of the corner of my eye I see him approaching.

'You're amazing,' he says. 'Ever thought of playing in a band?'

I keep my head down hoping he'll go away. He doesn't. I'm panicking now. List. What? Anything . . .

Cross stitch.

Blanket stitch.

Chain stitch.

'I'm Ryan,' he tells me.

Running stitch.

Zig-zag.

Tack.

'Maybe I could buy you a coffee or something?' He looks down at my violin case full of coins and grins. 'Or maybe you can buy me a coffee?'

I've run out of stitches. My silence doesn't stop him. He just decides I don't understand English.

He gestures drinking from a cup – he even crooks his little finger.

'Caf-e? Per fav-or-ay?' he says in a daft foreign accent.

I shake my head and bite my lip trying not to smile but it's too late – he's noticed.

'A nice cup of teeeee?' he says in a comic voice. 'Liquidised wombat juice?'

I glance up in surprise. He grins triumphantly, knowing I understand him.

'Look, I'm totally harmless, honestly. My name's Ryan Baxter. I live just round the corner. Everyone knows me . . . Look, I'll prove it.'

He looks round then waves and calls to a middle-aged woman browsing at a nearby stall. 'Hi there, Mrs Woollacott, how you doing? Mrs Woollacott?'

She stops in her tracks and slowly turns around to face him.

'You're looking . . . um . . . radiant today,' he tells her with a grin.

But the only thing she's radiating is a disapproving scowl. She heads straight towards us through the crowd, like a battleship under full steam. She sucks in her breath and clenches her teeth. 'If you and your friends make that God-awful racket in your garage again tonight, I'll send my Steven round,' she threatens ominously, before turning and marching off.

Ryan grins sheepishly at me then shrugs. 'My next door neighbour. Mrs Woollacott. Nice lady . . . Not a music lover.'

I stifle a smile.

'And Steven . . . her son . . . he lifts weights and likes wrestling.' He eyes my reaction but I put my head down and quickly pack away my violin.

'No . . . I'll be fine. Really. Don't worry about me. Got to suffer for our music, haven't we? Or at least she has. My band – The Damage, great name, eh? – is obviously not her cup of tea. We play minimalist R and B with emo-screamo overtones.' He pauses for a moment, then adds, 'So, going back to tea – there's a great café down on the beach.'

Alarmed, I shake my head, snap shut my violin case and quickly get to my feet. He looks disappointed.

'Well, you can't just go like this,' he says. 'Steven may tie me in a half nelson when I get home so we might never meet again. Think how you'd feel then.'

I pick up my case and hurry away.

'At least tell me your name!' he calls after me.

Chapter 15

Ellie

'Just don't say a word!' I order Grace, as she steps through the caravan doorway.

I don't have to worry. As I slowly unwrap the towel from around my head, she just stares at me with her mouth wide open.

'So it went wrong, OK?'

She nods slowly but still can't take her eyes off me. Neither can Bruno. I've hypnotised them both.

'It went totally and completely wrong and I don't know what to do! Will you both stop staring at me like that!' I snap angrily, tears splashing down my cheeks.

Grace looks down at her violin case. Bruno slopes off and lies on his blanket.

'I'm sorry. I didn't mean to shout at you, and I'm really sorry for everything I said earlier. Oh Grace, I hate my big mouth! I wish I could just zip it up and throw it away!'

She gives me a reluctant smile. 'You'd look pretty weird without it.'

'What am I going to do?' I wail.

It's a full five seconds before she speaks.

'Um . . . Don't suppose it'll wash out?'

'Nooooo! I've tried. I've washed it and washed it. It just gets more and more matted.'

Grace picks up the box and inspects the glamorous blond-haired girl on the front.

'I look just like her, don't I?!' I joke, burying my head in my hands as clumps of matted fluorescent-orange fuzz hang limply around my face. Bruno pads over to me, and gives my hands a lick, but my head's gone too weird for his liking – he gives my hair a couple of suspicious sniffs then retreats to his blanket.

'It's not that bad,' Grace says hesitantly. 'And bright hair's really trendy.'

'It's disgusting! I can't even comb it through; it's like felt. I can't go out with orange brillo pads dangling from my head. I'll have to stay here in this caravan for months, years . . . forever!'

I throw myself onto Gran's quilt spread over the bench and sob noisily. How long will it be before being forced to hide from the world in this tiny caravan sends me stark raving bonkers, just like Stan's wife?

Grace ignores me and disappears off into our little bedroom. She comes back holding her sewing scissors.

'What if I trim all the matted bits away? Maybe it won't look quite so bad then. Want me to try?'

'I don't care any more!'

'Sure?'

'Just do it! Make me bald – I couldn't look any worse!'

Grace takes a deep breath, makes me sit upright then gently starts to cut my hair. She takes her time, looking at my head thoughtfully as she snips away at the tangles, bit by bit. I stare down at the fluorescent fuzzball growing on the floor. Bruno looks curiously at us both but doesn't leave the safety of his blanket.

'I only wanted to be noticed, like you!' I tell her. 'Everyone notices you, Grace.'

'I so wish they didn't,' she replies softly.

Something in the tone of her voice reminds me that while I've been busy transforming my hair into radioactive candyfloss, she's been out for the last couple of hours.

'So where have you been?' I ask, curiously.

She pulls a face. 'You won't tell Mum?'

'Um . . . OK . . .' I'm worried now. Grace never does anything dodgy.

'I was busking.'

'Busking? Really?'

She nods shyly.

'Made about fifty pounds.'

'Grace. You're a genius!'

'Not quite . . . but nice to know all those music lessons haven't been a complete waste of money.'

'Dad would go ape if he knew!' I blurt out, before I can stop myself.

Grace tenses. A dark cloud suddenly hovers over us. I smooth Gran's quilt under my fingers, flicking a couple of clumps of hair onto the floor.

'But . . . hey, I bet our grandad wouldn't mind,' I start to babble. 'Yeah, he'd have said something like, "Go girl – you rock, big time!" Or whatever they used to say in the good old days. So did anyone dance?'

'Ellie, shut up,' she says with a faint smile.

But the suffocating black cloud has gone. We've blown it away.

'Weren't you nervous?' I ask.

She nods. 'Totally, at first, but then it was like the people watching just melted away and I didn't really notice them any more. Except . . .' She stops for a moment, thinking about something. Or someone.

'What?' I ask.

'Nothing.'

'Tell me . . .'

'There's nothing else to tell. It was great. I played just what I wanted. How I wanted. I felt . . . it sounds really stupid, but I felt free.'

When she's finished cutting my hair, I open the door to the little bathroom and peer cautiously in the mirror above the sink.

'What d'you think?' she asks.

'I think . . . I don't look like me any more,' I say surprised.

It's true. I don't. I run my fingers through my short tousled hair so it spikes out in places. With all the matted bits cut off, what's left is a bright but soft apricot instead of a horrible day-glow orange. Somehow the colour brings life to my skin and my eyes seem bigger – brighter even.

'I actually like it,' Grace tells me.

'Really?'

'Yeah. Looks funky. Suits you.'

I look again. I even find myself smiling. I've got rid of the old mousy Ellie that I've always hated and I'm looking at a completely different girl.

'Well say hello to the new me!' I tell her.

Grace shrugs, and says in a posh, silly voice, 'Oh hello, *Elle*.'

'*Elle!* Oh I really love that! Hey, will you call me Elle now? It sounds soooo much nicer than boring old Ellie.' I turn back to the mirror and pretend I'm meeting someone for the first time. 'Oh hey, yeah, my name's Elle.'

Reflected in the mirror, I see Grace behind me, rolling her eyes.

'I was joking,' she says.

'But I love it. Oh go on, Grace, call me Elle, please.'

'I'll forget.'

'Well, from now on, that's who I'm going to be. New hair. New name. New life.' I eye her mischievously. 'Want me to cut yours now?'

Chapter 16

Grace

We clip on Bruno's lead, then head back to town to get the rest of the shopping. I steer Ellie away from the market and towards the main street. She's positively bouncing as she walks along and keeps checking her reflection in shop windows. A group of boys about our age hanging around the bus shelter wolf whistle and laugh as we pass. One – really good-looking with dark hair and a lopsided cheeky smile – thumps his chest like Tarzan and calls after us, 'Hey girls, which one of you wants to go out with PJ?'

His mates laugh as we ignore them, but even though Ellie tuts at me disapprovingly, she can't quite hide the huge grin spreading across her face.

'Let's have a feast,' she announces impulsively, as we dive into the little supermarket wedged between the newsagents and a gift shop. 'A big, fat, totally calorific feast!'

'We need to save money, Ellie,' I insist, as she tosses expensive pizzas, a giant carton of luxury ice cream and a huge box of chocolates into our basket before I can stop her. 'Look, I've made a list of everything we need.'

'Pah! Life's too short for lists!' she retorts. 'Don't know why you're so obsessed with them.'

'I am not obsessed!'

'That's got to be the understatement of the century – I bet you've even got lists of all your lists!'

'Very funny.'

'And a list of your lists of lists. And a—'

'Shut up, Ellie.'

'Well, I'm right, aren't I?'

'No. You're just very irritating. Making a list keeps things under control, OK?'

'You sound just like Dad now.'

'No I don't!' I snap.

'Well, I want to be totally out of control for a change,' she retorts. 'Oh come on, Grace,' she pleads. 'Let it go. The chocolates are a treat for Mum . . . except the caramels, which she never eats.'

'Just half the box then.'

'Well . . . she won't mind if we have some too.'

'Suppose not.'

'What's the matter?' Ellie asks.

'Nothing.'

'You keep looking around . . . Is it those boys?'

'Course not!'

'That PJ was funny, wasn't he?'

'Let's just get the rest of the food and go.'

I can feel myself blushing and turn away so Ellie can't see my face, because I have been thinking about a boy – but not PJ. Ryan. And I'm annoyed, because for some stupid reason I can't stop thinking about him. I don't know what's got into me all of a sudden. I don't do boyfriends. Danny Kensell, next door, used to ask me out on a weekly basis. Other boys at school tried sometimes but always gave up pretty quickly because I never said a word.

This boy, Ryan . . . OK, he was funny and I even quite liked him, but I could never talk to him. Everyone who meets Dad thinks he's funny and likes him too.

You can't trust anyone – no one's really who they pretend to be. And some people are clever: they can flip from nice to nasty in the blink of an eye or the swipe of a fist, before you've even had the chance to say sorry or dive out of their way.

We get the rest of the shopping then untie Bruno who's been waiting patiently for us outside the little supermarket. As we head back to the caravan site, we don't see PJ and his mates or Ryan, but we pass other groups of teenagers hanging out together, laughing and joking, and I notice Ellie steal envious glances at them. I know she'd love to be with them, just larking about, because she still doesn't realise that it's better not to get involved, just in case.

Back in the caravan, Ellie insists on putting the pizzas into the oven and laying the table to surprise Mum. It's just gone five when we leave Bruno, and walk up to the café to meet her.

'What's she going to say about my hair?' asks Ellie anxiously.

We peer through the café window to see Mum busy clearing one of the tables. There are no customers now and the sign on the door says *Closed*. We go in and when she turns and sees Ellie hovering behind me, she jumps, nearly dropping the tray she's holding.

'Oh my goodness, Ellie! What have you done?'

'Does it look awful?'

'Well, no, but it's a bit of a shock – you look completely different!'

'But that's just what I want.'

'You should have asked me first, love; you've never used hair dye before – you could have had an allergic reaction or something. Grace, why didn't you stop her?'

How can anyone stop Ellie? I want to retort. It's easier to stop

61

a ten tonne runaway truck with a feather. But as usual I can't answer her, even to say it's not my fault.

'Oh Grace!' sighs Mum, throwing me a despairing look. And I know she's as upset with me as she is cross with Ellie.

'Grace wasn't there – I mean, she didn't know what I was doing because . . . I . . . um . . . locked myself in the bathroom,' Ellie says.

'So who cut your hair?'

'Well, she did. But that was after I dyed it . . . and I did ask her.'

Mum shakes her head. 'Honestly, you two! Thank goodness your dad —' She stops and bites her lip but we all know what she was about to say.

'How did it go today?' asks Ellie, quickly changing the subject.

'Great.'

'Where's Stan?'

'Had to go home early. Daphne's not well. I've been on my own all afternoon.'

I look around and see a vase full of bright yellow flowers on each table. But it's not just the flowers – the whole place looks fresher.

Mum looks different too. Straighter . . . taller somehow, but that, even by the standards of Ellie's overactive imagination, is impossible. 'I've been rushed off my feet,' she tells us with a huge grin on her face, 'but I haven't had so much fun for ages.'

When everything's tidy, Mum locks up, and we stroll back home. When we arrive at the caravan, she sniffs the air, puzzled.

'You haven't left the cooker on have you?' she asks. 'I can smell burning.'

'Oh no! The pizzas!' shouts Ellie.

We rush in and Mum turns off the oven but it's too late – all that's left inside are three charred black discs.

'It was going to be a lovely surprise!' wails Ellie.

'Well, it is . . . sort of,' Mum says with a nervous giggle. 'You haven't set the caravan alight. That's something.'

Again she amazes me. Back home something like this would have been a major trauma, something terrible to eradicate before Dad saw. Now it's just a few burnt pizzas and no harm done.

I glance down to see Bruno lying contentedly on his blanket next to the empty ice cream carton, busily licking off the last remnants of luxury fudge ice cream from his fur and looking extremely satisfied with himself. I'd left Ellie to put the carton in the little freezer compartment. She'd been so busy with the pizzas that she must have forgotten and I hadn't noticed either.

'We wanted a treat for you,' Ellie mumbles, 'and now everything's ruined.'

I pick up the box of chocolates from the floor and pass them to her. One corner of the cardboard is soggy and mangled where it's been half chewed by Bruno but apart from that the rest is undamaged.

Ellie opens the box then offers them to Mum, who smiles and takes one.

'You've got the brazil caramel!' says Ellie surprised.

'Delicious . . . thank you,' she replies, and I remember that they are Dad's favourites.

As we cook tea together, Mum drops a bombshell.

'On Monday, we need to go along to the school in town, see if they've got places and get you both enrolled.'

'We're going to go to school here?' asks Ellie shocked.

'Well, if we're staying, yes.'

'We are staying, aren't we?' Ellie asks anxiously, touching her hair. 'We're not going home?'

That horrible, old queasy feeling returns to the pit of my stomach.

'Do you want to go home?' asks Mum hesitantly, her voice quivering.

'No!' Ellie says.

'Grace, what about you?'

I shake my head.

'So, we're here. But you've got to go to school. Besides I'll be at work half the week. And goodness only knows what you'll get up to next, Ellie, if I'm not around.'

My heart sinks. I don't want to go home but apart from there, school's the last place I want to be.

Chapter 17

Ellie

'It's going to be fine,' I tell Grace, forcing my voice to sound confident. 'And because Dad's not here, we don't have to worry about Mum now. She's safe.'

School seemed like a fun idea yesterday, another new adventure, but now, in the cold light of day I'm petrified. What if no one talks to me or I end up on my own all day? What am I going to do? It'll be totally awful. I'm going to look like a right saddo. It's OK for Grace, she'll keep her head down and won't want anyone to speak to her, but I had enough of being a Billy No-Mates at my last school. It was horrible and I hated it.

We walk along the path past the stones, a shortcut up to the community college, wearing second-hand uniforms bought from a charity shop in town yesterday, after we enrolled that morning.

'Silly buying brand new,' Mum said cheerfully, as we picked out grey skirts, candy stripe green and white blouses, ties and dark green sweatshirts, 'no one'll even notice.'

I didn't say anything but Grace and I both knew that she didn't have the money for brand new stuff. Besides, Grace would look fantastic dressed in a bin liner and with a bit of luck, my new haircut and colour might just distract people from noticing my second-hand sweatshirt.

Just before we left the shop, Grace found a beautiful flowery top and got me to persuade Mum to try it on. She never usually wears bright colours but she looked absolutely lovely in it so I made her buy it and she even wore it home, giggling that she felt like a new woman. And she is. She laughs and smiles so much these days.

And now, as we walk through the stone circle, I stop at the tallest stone and place my palms on the front for good luck. The rock is cold and rough and wobbles just a fraction when I press against it.

'Do you think it's true – that they were once girls?' I ask Grace.

'Don't be daft.'

'But just imagine, you're dancing here on the grass with all your mates, not a care in the world, there's a massive bolt of lightning, it lights up the whole sky and suddenly – suddenly – you can't move, you can't talk – you can't do anything!'

I close my eyes and imagine I'm turned to stone, which isn't very successful because after a couple of seconds I can feel the collar of my shirt itching my neck and I give into scratching madly.

'It's just a story, Ellie. Something to frighten people with.'

'It's scary. This whole place is scary. Have you noticed how it's always so quiet?' I peer round at the circle of stones. 'Nothing but the Maids softly breathing . . . '

'Shut up, Ellie —'

I glare at Grace like a zombie.

'Elle – my name is Elle,' I say in a creepy voice but Grace isn't impressed.

'Great. We're going to be late on our first day . . . Elle,' she tells me, walking off.

'Wait for me!' I say with a shiver, hurrying after her.

66

We arrive at school just as the bell is ringing. Hordes of kids barge past us. Neither of us is sure where to go, so we follow signs saying *Reception*, where the woman behind the glass hands us our timetables and points us in different directions.

'Good luck then,' I say to Grace.

She nods back at me. 'You too.'

'Maybe you should try to speak to people here,' I say hopefully. 'It might help.'

Grace pulls a face. 'Maybe.'

'Things are different now, we've got a new start.'

She shrugs and I leave her, making my way down the packed corridor, until I find my form room. The room's noisy and crowded but as I stand awkwardly just inside the door, a pretty girl with long brown hair, loosely piled up on her head, passes me.

'You new?' she asks.

I nod and paste on what I hope looks like a friendly and not totally desperate smile.

'I'm Caitlin,' she announces. 'Like your hair.'

'Thanks. Like yours too.'

'Don't! It's supposed to be sophisticated but I can feel it flopping down into "muppet".'

We exchange a giggle.

'Muppets are cool,' I tell her.

'Well, they do have the best eyebrows —'

'Yeah, all curly – big hairy caterpillars —'

'I'm not wearing mine today,' she jokes in a theatrical whisper.

'I am! But don't tell anyone, they've just crawled off behind my ears.'

We giggle again and I know that this is the friend I've been waiting forever to find. There's an instant connection between us. We're on exactly the same wavelength.

I glance around the room and notice others looking over. 'My name's Elle,' I say, hoping I'm not pushing my luck.

I follow Caitlin to join another girl, Abi, and we sit down together as three more girls come over.

'Abs and me are best friends,' Caitlin tells me. 'And this is Ruby, Shareen and Freya,' she adds. 'Meet the lovely Elle, everyone.'

The other girls say hello.

'When did you move here?' Abi asks.

'Just a few days ago.'

'Where from?'

'London.'

'Cool. My cousin lives there,' says Shareen. 'She's got a really good job – earns a packet.'

'So where are you living now?' asks Freya.

'Um . . . oh, we're just somewhere temporary at the moment,' I say as all the girls look at me questioningly. I don't want to tell them we're living on a caravan site because we've run away from Dad. Before I can stop myself, I blurt out, 'till we can move into our new house.'

'One of those they're building up on the downs?' asks Ruby.

'Um . . . yeah, that's right.' I nod casually, not having the faintest idea where she means but hoping we can change the subject now.

'Wow! They're amazing, they are – one of them's got an indoor pool,' says Cait with a laugh. 'Help! I'm going green!'

Trust me to pick probably the most expensive houses in the area, I think, mentally kicking myself.

'So is it that one or the one next door with the tennis court?' Abi asks.

I kick myself again but keep smiling. Pool or tennis court? It's no contest – splish, splash, gulp, gulp. I'm already out of my depth. 'The one with the pool.'

'Yes!' says Cait, excitedly. 'Hey, when you've moved in you've just *got* to throw a big pool party, hasn't she?'

'Too right.'

'OK, sure.' My heart is sinking like a stone into my imaginary, luxury swimming pool.

'Hey everyone, this is Elle,' calls Cait to the rest of the class, 'and we're all invited to her party.'

Most of the others now turn around to look at me and a few of the boys give a cheer.

'Cait,' says Abs, 'she hasn't even moved in yet!'

'Yeah, and what about her parents? They might say no way,' adds Shareen.

'Oh, but they won't, will they?' pleads Cait.

I shrug. My imaginary parents definitely wouldn't say no.

'They're pretty cool about stuff,' I say.

'Wish mine were!' says Shareen, rolling her eyes. 'They're always on about something. "Tidy your room", "Do your homework", "Empty the dishwasher". They never stop.'

'That's cos they're both teachers,' says Ruby with a laugh. 'Nagging's in their blood.'

'Hey, we could have a theme – mermaids and . . . um, I don't know, fish or something – ask your dad tonight – then we can get planning.'

'Um, I can't,' I say, pulling a face. 'He's not around at the moment.'

'Why's that?'

My mind's racing. What can I say? I've never told anyone the truth about what happened at home and I'm not going to start now. I glance around the room, catching sight of a map of the world pinned on the wall. 'He's . . . abroad.' How far can I send him? Outer Mongolia? Antarctica? The moon? For goodness' sake, just make it convincing, Ellie, I tell myself.

'He's in America.'

'Really?'

'Yeah, he's been working out there for a few months now,' I say, slipping into my fantasy. 'I really miss him.' I give a sad little shrug for effect, although my thoughts are in a whirl. What on earth's he doing there? An image of Dad as a cowboy, complete with hat and horse, flits into my head. I immediately shove it out, but his 'always the drama queen' taunt rings in my ears.

'He's an actor,' I say impulsively.

Cait's mouth drops open.

'An actor, wow. That is the best. Is he famous?'

It's too late now. I can't contradict myself, or tell them I've just made everything up to impress them or they'll be furious. I have to stick to my story. Keep it real.

'No, but I suppose he might be one day. He's in a film. They liked his English accent. And his agent said although it's not a massive part, it's a really good one, so he shouldn't turn it down.'

Caitlin, Abi and the other girls are looking at me now as if I've just floated in on a golden cloud. Something's shifted — something small, but something important. Suddenly I'm not just a new girl, I'm somebody special, someone worth knowing.

The teacher hurries in and calls to everyone to settle down. In the scramble for seats, Caitlin and Abi both want me to sit next to them. I end up between the two of them, and we make whispered plans to sit together in all the classes we share and meet up at break and lunchtime. I'm barely listening to the teacher droning away. I am on a golden cloud. Cloud nine.

At my last school, because of Dad, I didn't really have any friends. I told white lies, made excuses and I got used to being the mousy, boring one — the girl who always melted into the background. And now it's really weird, again because of Dad and a few more porkies, suddenly I'm getting the chance to be the cool kid — the glamorous one, the one everyone wants to be friends with . . . and guess what? It feels great.

Chapter 18

Grace

I head down a maze of corridors and promptly get lost. When I eventually find my form room – a quarter of an hour later – and look through the glass door, I see a short, middle-aged lady in a beige trouser suit padding silently up and down between the rows of desks, addressing the class in quiet clipped tones. Unlike the room next door, where the teacher's raised voice can barely be heard over the bedlam, no one is even daring to whisper in here. I slip in at the back and sit down, hoping I won't be noticed.

'Ah, you must be Grace Smith,' the teacher announces immediately, as everyone turns around and stares. In amongst the blur of faces I spot two familiar ones – Ryan Baxter and that good-looking boy, PJ – before I quickly lower my eyes and stare down at the floor.

'You are Grace Smith, aren't you?'

Keeping my head down, I nod.

'I'm sorry? I didn't quite hear what you said.' There's a slight edge to her voice now.

I squirm on my chair, wanting to answer but unable to form the words.

'Well, Grace?' she growls, impatiently. I look up and we lock eyes. Hers are steely grey and she has two deep frown lines between them on her forehead.

'Late on your first day – not a very good start, is it?' she says softly.

I manage to keep eye contact but behind her back, I notice PJ mimicking her every word.

'I am Miss Turner. Apart from being your form teacher, I teach history. I'm also Head of Year Nine and in charge of discipline. So any problems or difficulties, you come and see me. Understood? My office is two doors down from the Headmaster's.' There's a pause. '*Yes, Miss Turner!*' she barks, staring at me.

My mouth is dry and I can feel that horrible queasy feeling welling up from the pit of my stomach.

'*Yes. Miss. Turner,*' she repeats slowly, as if I'm stupid. There's a deathly silence around me. Glances fire across the room like arrows. PJ's grinning like a Cheshire cat. Again I try to speak but my mouth is clamped firmly shut.

'Well, I'm not quite sure what you got away with at your last school, young lady,' she says looking at some paperwork on her desk, 'but here it's customary to reply politely to a teacher when he or she addresses you.'

I stare at Miss Turner. The sick feeling grows stronger. Everyone is watching, scanning my face and Miss Turner's, to see who will blink first.

'Maybe she's just shy, Miss,' calls a voice. It's Ryan.

'Baxter, when I want your input I'll ask for it.'

'But, Miss, it's only her first day —'

'Precisely. And Grace Smith is not the only pupil to swan into this school, thinking she can behave exactly how she likes. So right from day one – hour one, in fact – I'd like her to know that *Zero Tolerance* is my motto. What is my motto, Jacobs?'

'*Zero Tolerance*, Miss Turner,' PJ repeats.

'And the one thing, more than any other, that I will not tolerate is rudeness. By the way, you're in detention, Jacobs, I don't care to be lampooned.'

PJ's smile falls off his face.

'I haven't done nothing!'

'Double negative makes a positive. Lampoon. L–A–M–P–O–O–N. Look it up in the dictionary. From the library, if you don't possess one.'

Miss Turner turns and glares coldly at me once more and I feel as if I'm going to be sick any second.

'So, Miss Smith; what am I to make of you?'

I breathe deeply as I take in her stony-faced expression. I desperately want to explain that I'm not being rude but I can't, so she reads my silence as yet more defiance.

Four more seconds tick slowly by, until thankfully I'm saved by the bell. As everyone gets up to go to their first lesson, I turn and quickly follow them.

'I'll be on your case, Miss Smith,' I hear Miss Turner call after me. 'Make no mistake.'

Ryan is outside the classroom, waiting.

'Still alive?' he asks.

I look at him, grateful he tried to stick up for me.

'Even the Head's scared of her. Rumour is, she eats one little Year Seven kid for lunch every day then spits out the gristly bits in a bucket under her desk.'

I can't help smiling at his gruesome picture as I take out my timetable. Ryan glances at it.

'Set Two for maths with Mr Harris – me too. Come on.'

I follow him down the corridor.

'Hairy Harris is pretty harmless. Unless there's a full moon of course . . .'

Chapter 19

Ellie

Grace and I have been at school just over a week now and I'm not sure what Grace thinks because she hasn't said much, but I'm loving it to bits. I have friends! Real, true, lovely, funny, brilliant, wonderful friends! Out of them all, I still like Cait the best; she's so totally cool. She reminds me a bit of Lauren back home – except Cait's miles prettier and loads more fun. Everyone wants to be her friend, but since I've been here we've just clicked. We're best mates now – with Abs and Ruby, of course, and we always hang out together and giggle in class, sharing secrets – well, theirs not mine – but best of all she's invited me over to her house on Saturday. I can't wait!

This lunchtime, as usual, I'm sitting with them all on a bench in the playground, boy watching. I don't mention I'm not that interested in boys yet, except for the gorgeous PJ maybe. Anyway, most of the boys at my last school were just spotty oiks or complete aardvarks, but Abs says that some of the Year Nine boys here aren't bad, especially one in particular. She's bound to mean PJ; he's really popular but when he smiles at you it's like you're the only person in the world.

'Shut up, Abs!' says Cait, pushing her slightly and grinning madly.

'Well, he is really cute,' Abs tells me. 'All the girls fancy him. Not just Cait. . .'

'Abs, I don't fancy him!'

She doesn't, she's mad about some boy called Ryan.

'Yeah, but he fancies you too,' Ruby chips in. 'Daisy Millar says he's going to ask you out.'

'In your dreams!' says Cait with a big grin.

'He is too!' Ruby insists.

I'm just about to say I think PJ's really cute too, when Cait suddenly turns around and pulls a dramatic face.

'Oh no!' she says, her eyes widening. 'He's over there! Don't look! Don't look! By that big tree!'

I peer over towards the tree and immediately spot Grace, with a tall blond-haired boy. The famous Ryan.

'Who's she?' demands Cait, her mouth drooping.

Shocked, I don't answer.

'She's new,' Ruby says. 'Daisy told me she doesn't talk to anyone. I saw PJ try to chat her up yesterday but she just looked through him like he wasn't there.'

I shuffle uncomfortably from foot to foot. Although I think maybe I should say something, I'm angry with Grace. Why can't she just be normal for goodness' sake?

'Well, she'd better keep her paws off Ryan. He's taken,' giggles Abs.

Grace and the boy disappear around a corner.

'Come on, let's spy on them,' says Abs, getting up. On tenterhooks, I glance at Cait.

'Don't be such a saddo,' she says, as I breathe a secret sigh of relief. 'Anyway I want to go to the drama auditions. You coming, Elle?'

'Yeah, OK,' I say casually, desperate to get away.

'We're doing *Princess Caraboo*,' says Abs, as we a

75

to the hall together. 'Mrs Mulligan wrote it.'

'She totally ripped off the film,' Ruby adds dismissively.

'No she didn't!' protests Cait. 'It's a true story. It's about a beautiful, mysterious girl who turns up one night at this posh mansion and doesn't speak any English. She persuades everyone she's a foreign princess, but really she's just some servant girl called Mary Baker who's broke and starving.'

'Cait's going to be Princess Caraboo.'

'Except I haven't got the part yet, Abs.'

'Oh come on, like Mad Mulligan doesn't think the sun shines out of your rear end. Bet you anything it'll be your name top of the cast list next Monday.' Abs turns to me. 'She played Annie last year in the musical we did. She was in the paper and everything.'

As we reach the hall, we pass PJ leaning against the corridor wall, chatting with his friends.

'Hey, Caitlin, you coming to Dalti's party Saturday night?' he asks with that grin.

'What's it to you?' asks Cait all casual.

'Well, if you wear something halfway decent so you don't look like a drag queen for once, I might just take you.'

I look at him in surprise. His mates laugh and for a second Cait seems flustered and blushes bright red. PJ catches my eye and winks. Now I'm flustered too.

'She wouldn't go with you, if you paid her,' giggles Abs, grabbing Cait's arm and pulling her through the hall doorway. 'She's going with Ryan Baxter.'

'She paying him then?' PJ calls after us, setting off a fresh load of sniggers from his friends.

'Cheeky monkey!' says Abs.

'Don't take any notice of him,' says Ruby.

'As if I ever would!' Cait retorts, with a toss of her head.

walk up to the stage, and I'm trying to figure out PJ, d by Mad Mulligan herself, and I get the tiniest clue where her nickname came from. What is it with drama teachers? Why do they always look like they've got style tips from the high security establishment they've just escaped from? She's wearing purple dungarees, tucked into red boots, and a long-sleeved shirt in a fetching lime green. The whole look is set off by her scarlet lipstick and lashings of black kohl around her eyes.

'Just in time, ladies,' she says, ushering us towards a small group of girls waiting in the wing of the stage.

'I want to get our lovely Princess done and dusted before I sort out all the other parts. So who's this?' she asks, looking at me.

'Elle Smith, Miss,' I say.

'Her dad's a film actor in America.' Cait says.

'Really! Well, bit of competition for you lot then,' she says jokily, before I can explain that I wasn't actually intending on auditioning.

'You've got to have a go, Elle,' Ruby tells me. 'She's got to have a go, hasn't she, Cait?'

'Course,' says Cait generously.

We take it in turns to read out one of Princess Caraboo's speeches. Some of the girls, including Ruby, have no idea and don't put any meaning or the slightest bit of feeling into the words. They could be reading a bus timetable or names from a phone directory, but Cait is truly amazing and Mad Mulligan beams at her when she finishes.

'Glorious, Caitlin! Well done,' she says, pursing her red lips together and scribbling something down on her clipboard. Abs nods to me, and mouths 'Sorted'.

Soon there's just Abs and me left. Abs is not what anyone would call a natural actress and she knows it. She gets uncontrollable giggles on her second line, sets everyone else off and Mad Mulligan ends up stopping her.

'Good try, Abigail,' she says. 'OK, time's getting on – have a quick go, Elle, then we'll move on to all the other parts.'

As I step out onto the stage and begin reading, there's something about Princess Caraboo's situation that cuts straight to my heart. I know exactly what's going through her mind. Underneath all the confidence and blag she's totally fragile. She's plain Mary Baker, walking a tightrope, living a lie to survive.

There's silence when I finish. I look at Cait, Ruby and Abs' blank faces staring up at me and give an embarrassed shrug. I didn't think I was that bad.

'Thank you, Elle,' Mad Mulligan says, scrutinising me through her dark-lined eyes, then glancing back at Caitlin. 'OK. Right . . . well, I think that's Princess Caraboo in the bag. Let's move on to all the other parts.'

Chapter 20

Grace

'Detention, Miss Smith!' snaps Miss Turner.

Our relationship hasn't exactly blossomed since we first met. In fact, it's got steadily more pear-shaped over the last week, probably because I'm in her history class as well as registration so there are double the opportunities for her to pounce on me.

'You will take part in discussions the same as everyone else in this room,' she insists, glaring at me. Like a little grey-haired terrier with sharp pointy teeth, she just won't let go. She's been on at me throughout the whole lesson. The whole class is watching and waiting. No one's heard me say a single word so far.

'So, Grace, give me one method the Suffragettes used to try to persuade the government that women should get the vote. One method.'

If only I could speak I could give her ten. They:

Marched.

Petitioned.

Heckled.

Protested.

Disrupted.

Scuffled.

Burned.

Bombed.

Starved.

. . . and a few of them died too.

But I stay silent. My face is burning but I keep my head bowed and sneak a glance at my watch. My heart sinks as I see it's still ages till the end of the lesson.

'Deeds not words, Miss,' I hear Ryan call out from the back of the class.

'Don't shout out, Baxter!'

Ryan shoots his hand in the air. PJ and a few others grin or mumble under their breath, which doesn't go unnoticed by Miss Turner.

'I'm not interested, Baxter – put your hand down.'

'But Miss, that was the Suffragettes' slogan. *Deeds Not Words*. You gave Grace an A for her essay so maybe it doesn't matter whether she says anything in class.'

'Yeah, let's face it, wouldn't matter if she turned up at all, would it?' PJ calls out.

Miss Turner purses her lips as sniggers erupt around the room.

'If you're both so concerned about your fellow pupil, you may join her in detention tomorrow,' she snaps.

'Oh, Miss, come on, that's not fair!' retorts PJ.

'Life's not fair, Jacobs. And nor am I. We're both nasty, short and full of disappointment. Get over it.'

I bite my lip. If only I'd stuck to my usual tactic of dumbing down my work, Ryan couldn't have said what he did, PJ would have kept his mouth shut too and Miss Turner probably wouldn't be so interested in hearing my opinions.

I glance at Ryan and see to my surprise there's the trace of a smile on his face. I've spent most of the week trying to avoid everyone, especially PJ, but like Miss Turner, Ryan doesn't seem to want to give up on me.

'Don't let her freak you out,' he whispers the following afternoon as I follow him into the detention room, 'Just imagine her naked or on the loo.' He pulls a face. 'Actually, don't. Really. Don't. It's horrible. Not that I've ever seen her,' he adds quickly. 'I'm going to stop right there . . .'

I can't help but smile. Ryan looks at me, his face serious for a change.

'I love it when you do that,' he says. 'That thing with your lips . . . upwards . . .'

Reddening, I quickly turn away and sit at a single desk in the corner well away from PJ who hisses my name and pats the chair next to him. Miss Turner comes in, sets us all work, to be done in complete silence, then opens her laptop and starts furiously tapping away on it. I keep my head down and try to concentrate on the essay question in front of me but my mind's in a whirl and I can't stop thinking how Ryan is so different from all the other boys I know. Before I can stop myself, I'm scribbling a list on a scrap of paper.

Ryan

You're funny.
You stuck up for me.
You're thoughtful.
Kind.
Pretty smart.
But are you for real?

Suddenly, I catch him glancing over at me. Embarrassed, I quickly tuck the list inside my pocket, bow my head and hurriedly write my essay.

An hour later, after a long lecture on rudeness and how she's never yet let a pupil slip through the net, Miss Turner lets us go. I check my watch, relieved I've still got loads of time before Mum leaves the café. I made Ellie promise not to tell her I had a detention, because I know she'd be mortified.

Ryan catches me up and walks alongside.

'You all right?' he asks.

I nod, blushing slightly, as I remember the list in my pocket. PJ, hovering by the school gates, stares hard at us as we pass.

'Good . . . don't ever let Turner get to you, will you?' says Ryan.

We walk on up the road in silence.

'It's OK, you don't have to talk to me,' he says after a few minutes. 'I'm not going to make you.'

We take the road that leads up to the shortcut through the stones, and he tells me about a small cove further up from the main beach that can only be reached by boat, where he and his dad have fished for mackerel.

'There are seals too,' he says. 'I saw three pups this year. They were born in one of the caves that stays dry at high tide. Now they've grown, they swim out all the time. Proper little mermaids.'

I think about the seals we saw on our first morning, swimming around the rocks and wonder if they're the same ones.

'I could show you the place, if you like,' Ryan says as we approach the shortcut and see two girls sitting on a garden wall, their legs dangling. I recognise them both. They're Ellie's friends.

'Hey, Ryan, you going to Ben Dalton's party?' one of them calls.

The other girl digs her friend in the ribs, making her jump and smother a squeal.

'Yeah, course, he wants the band to play a few songs,' Ryan replies.

'We're going too, aren't we, Cait?' says the first girl, with a nod.

Cait gives a casual shrug.

'Might be,' she says, giving me a dismissive glance. 'Haven't decided yet.'

She looks up and smiles at Ryan, then twirls a strand of her long brown hair around her fingers. The other girl asks Ryan if he's asked anyone to go with him, and the three of them start chatting easily together. Feeling out of place, I take the chance to quietly slip away.

As I head down the path to the stones, Ryan calls after me. I turn and wave but now he's sitting on the wall between the two girls who are laughing and hanging on to his every word. Suddenly I feel a dull flat ache inside, different to anything I've felt before. Is this what jealousy feels like? I wonder. As I reach the stone circle, I distract myself by counting the stones, noticing the tallest one is leaning slightly backwards, as if the maid had been looking up to the sky when she was transformed. I tell myself I'm getting as bad as Ellie with her crazy imagination. Seventeen. Two more than last time. Puzzled, I start counting again when I hear a voice behind me call out.

'Hey!'

Thinking it's Ryan, I spin around, but I'm shocked to see PJ.

'Don't you know this place is haunted?' he asks.

I turn to go but he blocks my way. He's a lot taller than me and about twice as heavy.

'Everyone thinks you're weird cos you don't speak,' he says softly. 'Some people think you can't, but that's rubbish. It's all a big act, isn't it?'

He takes another step towards me.

83

'So what's your game?'

Unnerved, I take a step back but stumble against one of the stones, losing my balance and scraping my bare arm on its cold, rough surface. On seeing the thin dribble of red blood trickle down my wrist, PJ smiles that lopsided smile of his.

'Well, you're not alien, then,' he says, looking straight into my eyes. 'No green blood.'

I scramble to my feet, push past him and leg it.

'Maybe you're a ghost,' he calls after me. 'They don't talk either. Weird stuff happens here. But then you'd know that already . . . wouldn't you?'

Chapter 21

Ellie

'Where've you been?' I ask Grace as she hurries in.

'Detention. I told you.' She's out of breath like she's been running. She drops her bag, bends over Bruno so I can't see her face and gives him a cuddle.

'What's wrong?' I ask.

'Nothing.'

'They're only supposed to keep you an hour,' I remind her. 'What happened to your arm?'

'Scratched it on one of the stones.'

She grabs a tissue from the box on the table and dabs off some blood from the back of her hand.

'How come?'

'Just did. I was counting them.'

I can tell by her voice and the way she avoids my eye that she's hiding something. But unlike me she's a rubbish liar.

'Ellie . . . Stay away from that boy . . . PJ,' she says suddenly.

'Why?'

Her cheeks flush bright red. They always used to do that when Dad asked her a question and she didn't want him to know the answer.

'I don't like him.'

'You don't like anyone.'

'I mean it. There's something about him.'

'He's just a bit of a lad. I think he's quite funny, actually. And he's really good-looking. Probably the best-looking boy at that school.'

'Just keep away from him, OK?'

'Oh, so you're allowed to hang around with boys but I'm not. You're only one year older than me. That doesn't give you the right to tell me what to do all the time.'

We're heading for a full-scale row as the door clicks open and Mum comes in. 'Phew! Been on my feet all day long!' she says happily, hanging up her coat and chucking her bag under a chair. 'Good day at school?'

'Great,' I say as Grace turns away and starts to fill up the kettle at the sink.

'I'm so relieved you've both settled in – it can't be easy changing schools in the summer term, like this.'

'My friend Cait has asked me to her house tomorrow. I can go, can't I?' I ask.

'Don't see why not,' she says. 'I might be working again anyway. Poor Stan – his wife's been taken to hospital.' From her coat pocket she pulls out a piece of paper with a phone number scribbled on it. 'I promised I'd ring him.'

'What's happened to her?' I ask.

'She's had a fall.'

'Out of a window?'

'Don't think so,' says Mum, looking puzzled. 'Whatever gave you that idea?'

'Don't know . . . No reason.' Unless she'd finally flipped and gone completely bonkers, I think to myself.

It takes Mum a couple of hours before she plucks up courage and fishes in her bag for her mobile. Dad bought it for her a few years ago but she always kept it turned off which used to really annoy him because he couldn't check up on her if she went out. Everyone at school had mobiles except me (and Grace who for obvious reasons didn't want one) and I was dying to ask if I could have Mum's because she never used it. I waited until Dad was in a really good mood but he still went totally ballistic.

'With a voice as loud as yours, Drama Queenie, what the hell do you need a phone for? All you have to do is open a window and bawl your head off. The whole world will hear you.'

I didn't ask again, even when Christmas was coming up and he said I could have anything I wanted.

Mum looks at her phone nervously before turning it on. There are dozens of messages waiting.

Grace bites her lip.

'Don't listen to them, Mum,' I warn her.

'But there's so many!' she says, shocked. 'What if something's happened to him?'

'It hasn't. He's fine. He's always fine. Bad things don't happen to Dad. Mum. Please don't.'

But it's too late. She presses a key then holds the phone away from her ear as if it might bite her.

Dad's faint voice erupts into the room. First he's cross and impatient. 'So where are you, you stupid woman?' he demands. Then the tone changes and he's shouting and swearing at her, making all sorts of nasty threats. Bruno sits up alert on his blanket, gives a whimper then lies back down, his tail between his legs. In the third message, Dad's voice changes again. Now it's calm and so quiet we can hardly hear him, but this frightens me more than ever.

'I'll find you. You wait. I'll weed you out, and there'll be all hell to pay.'

With her head bowed, Mum quickly starts deleting all the messages. When she's finished, she looks up at our shocked faces.

'I'm sorry,' she whispers.

'He won't find us, will he?' I ask.

'No, course not,' she says, her voice shaking a little. 'We're safe here.'

But suddenly I don't feel safe any more. It's dark outside now and there isn't enough light from the few lamp posts spaced along the field to see anything more than a load of spooky shadows. But it's not ghosts appearing that I'm frightened of, it's Dad.

Mum doesn't ring Stan. She says she'll do it later and quickly buries the phone back in her bag as if it was a dangerous weapon. We start to make tea together but we're all jumpy and Grace accidentally drops a plate, smashing it to pieces. Mum says it doesn't matter and makes a joke of it but underneath her cheerful words, her voice sounds on edge.

I tell her we must get the mobile number changed and then only give it to school and people we want. She looks relieved and promises she'll sort it first thing tomorrow.

Every noise from outside sets us peering through the curtains and before we sit down to eat, Mum locks the caravan door, something she never usually bothers to do until bedtime. Grace leaves most of her meal and even I don't feel hungry. Although Mum tries to keep the conversation going, Grace is silent as usual and I don't feel like talking.

Suddenly there's a sharp bang on the caravan door.

I stifle a scream and Grace goes deathly white. Mum takes Bruno by the collar and pulls him towards the door with her and I can't help letting out a nervous giggle. The worst Bruno would ever do is lick someone to death, turning them into a sticky ball of dog drool. But he wouldn't dare do that to Dad.

There's a second thump. Louder. Heavier. None of us, including Bruno, move.

Chapter 22

Grace

'It's me!' a gruff voice calls from outside.

'Stan!' says Mum, taking a deep breath and unlocking the door.

'Didn't mean to frighten you,' he says, seeing our startled faces.

He steps into the caravan and stands awkwardly before us. He looks older and more grizzled than I remember.

'You've fixed the van up nice,' he says, glancing around. 'Looks homely.'

'Thanks. I'm sorry, Stan, I meant to ring you,' Mum says. 'How's Daphne?'

He wipes his hand across his face and shakes his head. 'Fifty years we've been married. Never a night apart till now.'

'I hope she'll be all right.'

Stan nods. 'I know it's your day off, but could you cover for me tomorrow at the café?' he asks.

'Of course, no problem,' Mum says quickly. 'I'll be there first thing.'

'Got the fishing club committee booked in the evening till

about ten, for their annual do – but I'll cancel them so you can close up normal time —'

'No, don't worry – it's fine. I've made pasties and quiches – they're in the freezer and I could do a seafood risotto and salad if they'd like.'

'They'll love it. You're pure diamond, Karin,' he says.

For a split second Mum's eyes well up and she looks like she might cry. She blinks and forces a smile. 'Just pleased to help,' she says.

He looks as if he's about to ask something but then just nods awkwardly, turns and goes, disappearing into the shadowy darkness outside.

It's late and Mum says it's about time we all got to bed. Even Ellie doesn't kick up a fuss, but half an hour later, lying in my little bunk, I can't sleep. I toss and turn but it's as if someone's put pebbles under the mattress. It's blowing a gale outside and the wind whistles noisily around the caravan, threatening to tip it over.

I think about PJ and try to convince myself that Ellie's right. Maybe he is just a bit of a lad. But there's something about him that makes me feel uncomfortable, on my guard all the time. I remember what he said about the stone circle being haunted and I shiver. Gran once told me that ghosts are only people from the past trying to find the ones they've lost. Just like Dad. It feels like he's haunting us.

I peek over the side of the bunk and in the moonlight see Ellie, also wide-awake, staring out of the tiny window watching the bare branches of the trees behind the caravan sway to and fro.

'You OK?' I ask.

'Sort of,' she replies. 'What do you think Dad's said to everyone back home?'

'Knowing Dad, as little as he can.'

'Think he'll make up a story about us being on holiday or something?'

'Probably.'

'But what about Auntie Anna?' she asks.

'He won't speak to her, he never does. Don't worry, Ellie.'

'I'm not,' she replies, but the sound of her voice says different. 'Night, Gracie.'

She hasn't called me that since we were little.

'Sleep tight.'

She turns over and snuggles down under the covers. After a few more long hours I'm drifting off but have horrible dreams about Dad sneaking into the caravan while we're all asleep, smashing everything up and attacking Mum. I wake suddenly. I'm sweating and I feel sick. It takes me at least a minute to calm down and reassure myself I was just dreaming, but then I lean over the side of my bed and discover Ellie isn't in the bunk below me. Terrified, I climb down and rush into the main room.

Hearing me clatter in, Mum switches on the light, her face alarmed. Ellie is tucked up next to her. She wakes too and rubs her eyes.

'Bad dream?' Mum asks gently.

I nod.

'Join the club,' she says, with a nod to Ellie.

I climb into bed with them both. It's a huge squash and I'm half hanging off the edge but I don't care; there's no way I'm going back to my bunk to be on my own. Mum tucks Gran's quilt over the three of us and I try and get the slightest bit comfortable.

None of us can sleep, so after about an hour lying there with Bruno pawing to get in too, Mum gives up and turns the light back on. She makes hot chocolate for Ellie and me, even though we've cleaned our teeth and are never allowed drinks in bed. We sit squashed together under the quilt, sipping the hot chocolate, listening to the wind outside. None of us wants to think about Dad.

'Has Stan really been married for fifty years?' Ellie asks finally.

'That's what he said,' Mum says.

'But have you ever actually seen Daphne?'

'No.'

'Isn't she allowed out?'

'How do you mean?'

'Well, if she was mad or something Stan would have to keep her locked up, wouldn't he?'

'She's not mad, Ellie, and even if she was mentally ill, he wouldn't lock her up!'

Ellie thinks for a moment. 'Then, you know how Dad didn't like you going out?' She won't look at Mum and I can't either.

'Mmm,' says Mum quietly.

'He used to make you stay in the house all the time. Do you think it's the same with Daphne and Stan?'

'Not all men are like your dad, sweetheart.'

Ellie pulls a face. 'So what was your dad like?' she asks.

'Grandad? He . . . he was . . . an amazing man.' Mum stares down at a patch of soft blue and red checked cotton, cut from a man's shirt.

'Gran told me once he wasn't born here, but I can't remember where she said he was from,' Ellie says.

'Czechoslovakia.'

'So how did they meet?'

'On a boat.'

'A boat! But Gran hated boats! What was she doing on a boat?'

'She was seventeen and had been on a school trip to France. She was sitting on some steps, feeling seasick.'

'Just like me – I really hate it when it's rough —'

I glare at Ellie; I want to hear the story. Mum never talked about Gran and Grandad back home because Dad would get annoyed and tell her to shut up. He never talked much about his own parents either, except to show Mum up, because they had been so totally wonderful in every way.

'So what happened?' Ellie asks.

'Well, Grandad saw her and felt sorry for her. He was nineteen, a student. He didn't speak a word of English but he played his violin to take her mind off how she was feeling and Gran said it was love at first sight. Somehow they managed to keep in touch and a few years later they were married.'

'Wow,' says Ellie. 'That's so romantic. And he played the violin, just like Grace!'

'He played the same violin. Gran gave it to me after Grandad died. She always hoped one of you would learn to play it.'

An excited shiver goes through me as I realise I've been playing my grandad's violin. I suppose Mum never said, in case Dad objected, for some stupid reason.

'But why didn't he go back home to his own country?' asks Ellie.

'He couldn't.'

'Why not?'

'Well – I don't know the full story, only what Gran told me, but in the seventies, no one was allowed to criticise the government there. You could disappear for good if the secret police had your name on their list. Grandad got caught up in student protests but he also played in a band – in secret, because they weren't allowed to play publicly.'

'Why?'

'I suppose the authorities thought if people listened to forbidden music they might start listening to forbidden ideas too. Anyway, one evening, he was just about to go out to play at a really important concert when his dad stopped him and warned him to stay at home because the police knew about it and were going to arrest everyone. Grandad, being Grandad, didn't listen but later that night, as he walked through the woods to the barn where the concert was going to take place, the police were waiting, just as his father had said. They saw him with his violin, recognised him and gave chase but he managed to give them the slip.'

My heart is in my mouth.

'What did he do?' asks Ellie.

'He knew he couldn't go home so he walked and hitchhiked to Austria. All he had were the clothes he was wearing and his violin. He was exhausted and starving when he finally got there and spent months in a refugee camp. Eventually he was allowed to come to England. And it was on that boat that he met Gran.'

'He was really brave, wasn't he?' Ellie says quietly.

Mum shakes her head. 'He didn't see it that way. He even stopped playing his violin here, because he felt he'd let his friends down by running away.'

'But he had no choice!' Ellie protests.

'That's what Gran told him, but he just said he'd lost his voice.'

Outside the storm has calmed and it's quiet except for the sound of an owl hooting. I look again at the ordinary piece of red and blue check fabric and think about my extraordinary grandad. Suddenly I feel very proud but totally sad rolled into one and wish that he hadn't died when Mum was only eleven.

'Let's try and get some sleep now,' she tells us. And it feels good to lie under Gran's quilt together, safe and protected from the darkness outside.

Chapter 23

Ellie

I wake up from dreaming about Grandad being chased by secret police who all look like Dad. It's gone half ten. Mum must have left for the café hours ago. There's a note on the table, written in her neat, sloping handwriting, asking us to make sure Bruno has a walk or two, hoping that I have a nice time at my friend's house and telling us not to get into too much trouble before she gets home from the café tonight.

Bruno is sitting patiently in front of the caravan door, in the hope that staring at it will magically dissolve a dog-shaped hole for him to jump through to freedom. Grace is still fast asleep under Gran's quilt and it seems mean to wake her after last night, so I pull on my jeans and top, scribble another note under Mum's, telling her I haven't been kidnapped, that I'm just taking Bruno out.

I plan on going down to the beach but Bruno has other ideas. He picks up the whiff of a rabbit and starts pulling me towards the path to the stones.

'Slow down!' I tell him, but I'm wasting my breath – he's obviously on a mission.

At the clearing, he zigzags from bush to bush sniffing furiously.

'Hello there!' I hear a voice call, and swing around to see Susan sitting cross-legged on a tartan rug spread on the grass in front of one of the stones, her computer on her lap. 'It's, um . . .'

'Elle,' I tell her.

'Elle . . . and Grace, that was your sister's name, wasn't it?'

I nod.

'I didn't recognise you at first. Like your hair! '

'Thanks,' I reply.

'I often come here to write,' she says. 'It's always so quiet, and on some days, I'm sure I can feel a sort of energy coming from the stones. But that's just daft, isn't it?' She adds with a laugh.

Seeing the opportunity of being petted by a friendly stranger, Bruno bounds over and introduces himself.

'Bruno!' I say sternly as he tries to lick the poor woman to death. 'Stop it!'

'It's OK. I like dogs. And you're lovely,' she tells him, which encourages him more.

I gently pull Bruno away.

'How's the book going?' I ask.

'So-so. Haven't pinned down the main character in this story yet. Something's missing.'

'Maybe she could be swapped by fairies and brought up by human parents or something,' I suggest.

'Like a changeling?'

'Yeah . . . I'd read a story like that.'

'Mmm. Me too.' She thinks for a moment. 'You know how people used to try and find out if their child had been substituted by fairies?' she asks.

'They'd check for wings or something?'

'Stan told me they'd put a shoe in a bowl of soup in front of the baby, and if it laughed — which meant it understood the joke – then they'd know for sure it was a fairy.'

'But what if it just laughed anyway? Some babies are really happy all the time.'

'Good point. Mmm, not sure Stan knows a great deal about babies. Anyway, hopefully it didn't happen too often because I've also read that if parents thought they had a changeling on their hands they'd dangle it over a fire to drive the fairies out.'

'Eurgh! Poor thing! But I'd make my changeling clever – one step ahead, all the time. She'd know exactly what to do to convince everyone she was a human child.'

'Sounds like a brilliant idea. Maybe you should write it.'

I can't help pull a face.

'I'm not a proper writer like you – it would just turn out rubbish.'

'You don't know that, until you try.' She delves into her big canvas bag and takes out a notebook with a purple patterned cover. 'Here. This one's spare. Write your story.'

'Really?'

'Ideas are what matters. And you've obviously got loads. Pick the best ones and weave them together into a magic carpet. You can go anywhere then.'

I take the notebook. 'Thanks.'

'You can let me read it if you want . . . when you're ready, of course.'

'OK,' I say hesitantly, remembering Dad's scornful reaction to my Araminta stories, 'as long as you don't laugh.'

'Why on earth would I do that?' she asks, puzzled. 'Unless you meant it to be funny, of course.'

I nod. 'Thanks . . . I better go.'

I hurry back to the caravan, clutching the book, already thinking about my first chapter.

Grace is sitting at the table writing another of her dumb lists, in between munching on toast, and I just catch the name *Ryan* written neatly at the top, before she stuffs the scrap of paper into her cardi pocket.

'Cait fancies him too,' I tell her.

'Don't know what you're talking about,' she says sniffily, eyeing my notebook. 'Where d'you get that?'

As I feed Bruno, then wash my hands, I tell her about meeting Susan and how I'm going to start writing again.

'You should,' Grace tells me. 'I used to love your stories.'

'You did?'

'Yeah. They were brilliant.'

Grinning, I pour out some cereal, slosh milk on top, grab a spoon and tuck in. Bruno hovers around my legs hoping to hoover up anything I might spill. I used to be a really messy eater at home – somehow peas would ping away from my fork or soup would slop off my spoon just before I managed to get it safely into my mouth. Dad insisted I did it on purpose but I really didn't; he just used to make me nervous, watching my every move.

After breakfast, I open the notebook and see an unwritten postcard of the stones lying on the open page. Susan must have tucked it inside and then forgotten about it. I put it to one side and get stuck into my story.

'Thought you were going to your friend's,' Grace says after a little while.

'I am, but not till three,' I tell her, scribbling away furiously.

'It's already gone two,' she says.

'You're joking!'

Tucking the postcard back in the notebook, I look down at my plain top and jeans. Cait has only ever seen me in my school uniform. I bet she wears really trendy clothes on weekends. What's she going to think of me like this?

'What's the matter?' Grace asks.

'What am I going to wear?'

'Um . . . what you've got on?'

'But I look a mess!'

'You look like Ellie.'

98

'*Elle*. My name's Elle.' I tell her crossly.

'Sorry. So what does *Elle* wear?'

'Not this!' I wail. I look at Grace who's rolling her eyes and have an idea. 'Could I borrow something of yours? Pleeeease!'

'OK,' she says with a shrug. 'What did you want?'

'Well, I have to look special . . . glamorous.'

'You got the right sister?'

'Oh Grace, shut up! You always look fantastic. You'd look good with a brown paper bag over your head.'

'Maybe I can find you one of those then,' she says with a smile.

We go into the little bedroom and half an hour later I'm standing in front of her in the pretty tunic dress she made a few months ago, cinched in at my waist with a leather belt intertwined with shells, black leggings and pumps.

'What do you think?'

Grace doesn't reply but adjusts the tunic, and puts a long necklace of shells around my neck.

'Grace!'

'Mmmm . . . pretty good. I should do this for a living.'

I poke her gently in the ribs.

'Ow!'

'Thanks,' I say, as I get going.

'See you later, Elle!' she replies.

Chapter 24

Grace

The tide is low. The beach seems to have expanded, as there's now about a mile of pale golden sand around me, the most I've seen since we've been here, all washed smooth and ironed flat by the sea. At the far end, near the café, there are a few families armed with buckets and nets searching the rock pools. The wind's chilly. I pull my cardi tightly round me as I watch a bunch of surfers paddle their way out to sea and then wait before leaping upright onto their boards to ride the best waves back to the shore.

I let Bruno off the lead and he runs around like a crazy dog, barking at seaweed and generally going bonkers. He splashes into the sea and I follow him to the water's edge as one of the surfers glides towards us.

It's Ryan. His face lights up when he recognises me. He steps off his board into the shallow water a few metres away from where I'm standing.

'Grace!'

I smile at him and he grins back. He comes over and makes

a huge fuss of Bruno, telling us both how brilliant he is. Bruno pays back the compliment by rolling over onto his back, his legs waggling in the air. With their friendship firmly cemented, Ryan turns to me.

'Come on. I can show you the seals. They're out by the cove.'

He picks up his board, tucks it under his arm and takes my hand in his. It's freezing cold but I don't mind.

He dumps his board with two surfer friends who are sitting further up the beach, then we walk up towards the cliff path with Bruno leading the way, his nose to the ground, sniffing intently.

'The cove's just over there,' Ryan tells me, pointing to a rocky outcrop.

We carry on walking for another ten minutes but I'm alarmed as I realise the path is getting nearer and nearer to the cliff edge. Worse still, it has big chunks missing where the ground has subsided, like bites taken out of a giant sandwich. Unlike Ellie, who would swing from the top of Big Ben for a laugh, I've never been good with heights; they make me dizzy and desperate to cling tightly to the nearest solid object, which right now happens to be Ryan.

Finally we stop and look out to sea but the only thing separating us from a drop of twenty metres is a frighteningly wimpy length of droopy wire. I can hardly bear to look at the shingle cove below us but as I reel back, I get a glimpse of what looks like the entrance to one of the caves.

'You OK?' asks Ryan as we sit down on a bench well away from the cliff edge.

I nod, thankful I didn't do anything really stupid like panic or faint. I'm embarrassed as I realise I'm squeezing Ryan's hand so hard he's trying not to wince. I loosen my grip, feeling hot and flustered, pull off my cardi and take a few deep breaths. Sitting at this safe distance, we watch the sea intently. After a few minutes, a seal emerges from one of the caves, encouraged by another who stays close by. The water is rough and choppy and the smaller seal has a job to swim against the strong current, which tries to carry her away from the rocks and out to sea. Suddenly she disappears completely. I scan the water but she's nowhere to be seen. Finally, she bobs up above the surface a good ten metres away from where she went under, then, fighting hard against the current, makes it to the rocks. The other seal climbs up, nuzzles her for a few seconds then the pair settle down side by side in the sunshine . . . sunbathing.

We're so busy watching them I forget all about Bruno, but when I do reach down to pat him, he's gone. I look around expecting to see him, nose stuck to the ground on the scent trail of a rabbit, but there's no sign of him at all. Suddenly there's a yelp from inside a large gorse bush growing by the wire fence, followed by scrabbling sounds, then a frightened whimpering.

We rush to the fence and peer over to see Bruno, several metres below on a narrow ledge, looking up at us pitifully as he tries to paw his way back up the cliff. But there's no way he's going to be able to do it without help.

'Wait here,' Ryan tells me, and before I can stop him he's climbed over the wire fencing. I watch petrified as Ryan edges down the rocks towards Bruno, who wags his tail faster as he approaches. Finally, he drops safely down onto the ledge next to Bruno. Ryan speaks softly, gently reassuring him, as he carefully runs a hand over his head, back and paws, checking for injuries.

'I think he's OK,' he calls up to me.

My heart's in my mouth as he gently picks up Bruno and lifts him onto a higher ledge, telling him to stay as he climbs up after him. I breathe a sigh of relief as Bruno does as he's told, thankful to Ellie for secretly trying to train him even though Dad labelled him the stupidest mutt in the world. Dad was wrong, as Ellie and I always thought. Bruno isn't stupid at all, he just instinctively knows who he can trust.

Bruno is first up over the cliff edge and I quickly grab his collar and clip on his lead, tying it around a fence post so he can't go anywhere. Ryan isn't far behind but suddenly he misses his footing and slips, dislodging a football-sized rock, which tumbles all the way down to the beach, landing with an ominous crash.

I stifle a scream as he grabs hold of a scrubby bit of bush and manages to stop himself sliding any further.

He looks up at me. 'It's OK, I'm good,' he says, but his face is contorting in pain and he doesn't attempt to move.

Trying not to look down, I drop to the ground, as close to the edge of the cliff as I can bear. Lying flat on the grass I lock my arm around the nearest concrete post then, hanging on for dear life, wriggle closer, leaning over the cliff edge, holding out my other arm for Ryan to grab hold of.

He reaches up and grasps my hand tightly then awkwardly heaves himself up over the side of the cliff and onto the grass.

He doesn't move for a minute. His face is as white as paper. Then he looks me straight in the eye and a crooked smile appears on his face.

'Hey, don't worry . . . I bounce.'

Chapter 25

Ellie

Cait's house is easy to find. She told me it was the blue one with the pale green window frames, down by the harbour. I was expecting a little fisherman's cottage but it's much grander, with palms and gravel in the front garden and looks like one of those posh houses you'd see in some glossy magazine. Dad would be impressed. Nervously, I ring the bell and wait. After a few seconds Cait opens the door.

'Elle! Come in.'

She's wearing jeans and a T-shirt. Suddenly I feel over-dressed.

'Love this!' she says gently touching the hem of my tunic. 'Where did you buy it?'

'Um . . . back home, ages ago.'

'Who is it Caitlin?' I hear a woman's voice ask.

'My friend, Elle,' she calls back, and suddenly I'm glowing with pride. Not only did I never invite people back to my house, nobody ever asked me to theirs either.

The walls of the hallway are covered with beautiful paintings and Indian rugs and everything looks very expensive.

'Wow,' I can't help saying.

'Not as nice as your new house,' Cait replies with a laugh. 'And we haven't got a pool – just a fish tank!'

I force a smile. We go up to her room and are busy chatting when her Mum comes in carrying a tray.

'Thought you'd like some juice and biscuits,' she says. 'What a beautiful dress, Elle.'

'Thanks.'

'She got it in London.'

'It's lovely. Really stylish. Cait, have you shown Elle all your dolls yet?' she asks.

'Mum!' Cait says, her face reddening.

'Oh, they're lovely Elle – she's got a whole collection.'

'Can you go please?' asks Cait, dying with embarrassment.

'You are funny,' says her mum. 'I bet Elle would love to play with them.'

Unconvinced, I nod politely.

'Has Dad put credit on my phone?' asks Cait, quickly ushering her mum out of the room.

'He's just doing it now, darling.'

'Thanks. Bye then.'

As she shuts the door on her, Cait turns to me. 'Thought we could meet Abs down the beach or somewhere.'

'Oh OK, great,' I say, trying to hide my disappointment. Despite the weird doll thing, and the playschool juice and biscuits, I loved being with Cait in her house.

'It's soooo boring here. Specially with Mum and Dad breathing down my neck all the time,' Cait moans, popping half a biscuit into her mouth. 'Eurgh, raisins! I hate raisins! They're like rabbit droppings.'

I giggle but eat mine all the same.

'You won't tell anyone about my dolls, will you?' she adds.

I shake my head. 'Course not.'

'I don't play with them now but when I was little I was so

desperate for a sister I used to pretend that's what they all were. Totally sad, but there you go.'

We've just finished everything on the tray when there's another gentle tap and a man cranes his head around the door.

'Here you are, Princess,' he says, gently throwing Cait a mobile phone.

'Dad!' she says. 'I could have dropped it!'

'As if you would.' He turns to me. 'So this is the famous Elle? I hear your dad's an actor. . .'

'Um . . . yeah,' I say nervously, gearing up to fend off any awkward questions.

'Our Caitlin's heading for fame and fortune too. Aren't you, Princess? She's really talented. Gets it from me, obviously.'

'Dad, go away!' Cait says, cringing again.

He does . . . but singing at the top of his voice.

'Let's get outta here!' wails Cait in a fake American accent, as she rolls her eyes theatrically.

But I can't help feeling she's lucky to have a dad who thinks she's so wonderful.

As we make our way up the street, she texts Abs who immediately texts back to say she'll meet us in five minutes outside the baker's.

She's already waiting when we arrive. Chilling out with friends on the weekend is something totally new to me but I don't want either Cait or Abs to realise how sad my life's been up to now. We head down the high street, then take the path to the beach and sit on the sand, chatting and giggling. I'm determined that I'm going to enjoy every single precious minute. Cait and Abs are full of talk about Ben Dalton's party this evening and ask if I want to come.

'Yeah, love to,' I say.

'We could knock for you,' Cait tells me.

'No, I'll meet you there.'

But they're not put off.

'So where exactly do you live?' asks Abs.

They're both looking at me now. What do I say?

'Up behind the beach,' I tell them vaguely.

I suddenly realise my big mistake – there are no houses there. Cait quickly twigs this.

'Not on the caravan site?'

Both of them are staring at me in surprise.

'Why didn't your mum rent somewhere nice in town?' Abs asks.

My brain's whirring and I can feel my palms sweating. What can I say? If I don't make it good, everything will be ruined. Suddenly I'm inspired.

'Because . . . well . . . she's a writer.'

'No!'

'Really?'

Both Abs and Cait look suitably impressed.

'Yeah. She's researching her next book and the main character lives on a caravan site a bit like this one. So it's the perfect place to soak up the atmosphere and get all the details right – well, for her anyway. . .' I roll my eyes and tut as if it's all a big hassle.

'Blimey,' says Abs with a laugh. 'Don't fancy that.'

'Oh, I do,' says Cait. 'I'd love to live in a caravan. But it's got to be one of those old-fashioned gypsy ones, like a wagon, all painted in bright colours. And I'd cook outside over an open fire, with a kettle hanging on a chain, and I'd lie in my little bunk at night, staring at the stars. It would be totally wonderful.'

'Not if you've got three smelly brothers and a dog with a bottom problem,' Abs grumbles. 'Sounds like hell.'

'Well, she hasn't, have you?' Cait turns to me and I shake my head. 'And it won't be for long, will it, cos your new house'll be ready soon.'

'Yeah, I don't mind slumming it for a while,' I reply.

'So has your mum written loads of books?' asks Abs.

'Tons,' I say vaguely. 'She's always got a whole bunch of new ideas up her sleeve. Says she weaves them all together and she can go anywhere – like on a magic carpet.'

'Can we meet her?' asks Cait excitedly, jumping up from the sand.

'Yeah, course, but, um . . . she's writing at the moment. She needs peace and quiet so she can concentrate. She doesn't like being disturbed,' I say, as to my horror I suddenly spot Grace, Bruno and that boy Ryan from school, on the cliff path.

I move round in an attempt to stop Abs and Cait noticing them, but I'm a second too late. Cait glances up and pulls a face and Abs makes a tutting sound with her teeth.

'What is it with that girl? She's always hanging around Ryan,' she complains, staring at them.

My heart is thumping as Grace looks down in our direction and I know she's seen me.

'Who does she think she's staring at?' mutters Cait. She turns and looks at me suspiciously for the first time. 'Do you know her or something?' she asks.

'No,' I mumble, shaking my head.

That one little word falls out of my mouth like a drop of poison, filling the air with an invisible deadly gas. I feel a tightening sensation in my throat. I've told a lorry load of porkies recently, but this tops everything. What sort of person wipes their own sister out of their life?

I've still got a chance to put everything right but then I realise if I tell them the truth, they'll drop me like poop on a scoop and I'll have no friends again. I can't bear the thought of this.

'She lives on the caravan site,' I say, unable to stop the words flying out of my mouth.

'Let's go,' says Cait, linking her arm in mine.

The three of us turn our backs on Grace and Ryan and walk down into town, but I feel flat, and Cait is sulking. To cheer her up, I spend the last little bit of money I have on ice creams. We walk around the shops carrying cones filled with huge scoops of fudge ice cream covered in chocolate sprinkles, my all time favourite, but we must have bought them from the wrong kiosk because the ice cream tastes bland and powdery on my tongue and the fudge pieces get stuck between my teeth like bits of grit.

Chapter 26

Grace

I watch Ellie disappear off with Cait and her friend and let out a sigh. Out of all the hundreds of girls at our new school that Ellie could possibly have made friends with, she had to pick the two that would most like to vaporise me. I'm wondering exactly what Ellie's told them about us as Ryan glances at me.

'Think I've hurt my arm,' he says, wincing in pain. We use my cardi as a makeshift sling before heading down to the beach where his mates promise to take his surfboard.

He lives down near the market in a little terraced house. The small front garden is full of bikes and the wreckage of bikes, homemade go-carts and old battered body boards, propped against the garden wall like tombstones.

'Home sweet home,' he announces as he pushes open the tatty front door.

'Hi, Dad!'

'What time d'you call this?' a voice calls from the kitchen.

'Sorry. Had a bit of an accident.'

A man in an electric wheelchair appears in the kitchen doorway.

'You OK, son?' he asks anxiously.

'Fine. Just fell down a cliff,' Ryan jokes. 'This is Grace, by the way. And Bruno.'

Ryan's dad looks flustered. 'Nice to meet you.' He takes off the makeshift sling and carefully checks Ryan's arm.

'It's OK, Dad, it's loads better now – probably just a pulled muscle,' Ryan reassures him.

'Promised me he'd be back this afternoon to take Harry and Tom to the park for a kick about, not fall down cliffs,' his dad grumbles to me.

'Well, I'm here now. And I'm all right,' Ryan says as two boys of about five, identical as peas in a pod, clatter downstairs and launch themselves onto him.

'I'm hungry!' says one of the boys, clinging onto Ryan's shoulders like a human limpet while the other sets about petting Bruno, who takes the smothering calmly in his stride.

'OK. Let's just fast-forward to tea. So what's it to be?' Ryan's Dad asks, going over to the fridge and flinging it open.

'Sausages!' the twins chorus.

'Well . . . all right then, if you're sure,' Ryan's Dad says. 'Sausages it is. . .'

I sneak a secret peek in the fridge and spot five or six packets of sausages piled on the shelf and not a great deal else.

'Get that pan down for me, will you, Grace?' he asks as if I'm just one of the family. Twenty minutes later, with us all helping or getting in the way, five plates of sausage, egg and tomatoes with a towering stack of bread and butter on a wooden board, are placed on the little table in the middle of the tiny kitchen.

'Well, sit down, Grace,' Ryan's Dad tells me. 'Sit down and tuck in or the gannets'll have every last mouthful.' He smiles at his boys then suddenly looks concerned. 'Ryan,' he says sternly. 'Cloth!'

Ryan looks at him bemused. 'Cloth?' he mouths.

111

'Tablecloth. From the drawer.'

Ryan throws me a look but does as his dad asks. He rummages about in the painted dresser in the corner, finally taking out an old faded tablecloth with a Christmas tree pattern printed round the edge. There's a bit of commotion as all the plates and cutlery are pulled off, the cloth is spread carefully on the table and everything is put back.

'That's better,' says his dad with a nod, wheeling himself up to the table and lifting one of the twins onto his lap so there's a chair spare for me. 'Don't want your friend thinking we're complete Neanderthals.'

I smile at him.

'Well tuck in. We do a pretty mean fry-up in this establishment.'

There's talking and eating and running around the table and ketchup spilling and being wiped up, and furious debates about which team's better – Manchester United or Chelsea – and whether there are dinosaurs living under the twins' beds and how many are plant-eaters and how many are meat-eaters and in all the chaos, it doesn't seem to matter one bit that I'm totally quiet, because with the four of them there's already more than enough racket going on. And I remember all the meals at home where Ellie, Mum and I sat up straight on tenterhooks, while Dad complained about the food and lectured Mum on how she should have cooked it, and think how different Ryan's dad is compared to mine.

Within fifteen minutes almost everything has been wolfed down. Ryan's dad catches me looking curiously at the twins and Ryan as they polish off the last of the loaf of bread.

'Growing lads, you see,' he explains. 'Hollow legs. Can't fill 'em fast enough.'

After tea, Ryan and I take Harry and Tom outside into the tiny backyard where they play excitedly with Bruno.

'They'd love a dog,' Ryan tells me. 'I just heard them

planning to kidnap Bruno and hide him in their bedroom later.'

The back gate opens and the two lads from the beach come into the garden. The taller, spottier one's carrying a bass guitar, the other has Ryan's surfboard which he props against the fence.

'Jacko can't play tonight,' he announces. 'His mum's grounded him.'

The other lad sniggers but Ryan looks aghast.

'You're joking!' he says. 'What we going to do?'

'Play the same old stuff . . . even more rubbish than usual?' says the first boy with a shrug.

'It's not funny, Darren – we're going to look like right numpties!'

'What's new?' asks Darren with a whiff of hopelessness.

'What d'you mean?'

'Well, all this screaming Emo-Screamo stuff . . . it's . . . it's doing my head in.'

'But it was your idea!' Ryan tells him.

'Yeah, but only cos it's easy. I only know three chords. And when Kev gets going no one clocks he's tone deaf.'

'I am not!' Kev protests. 'Year Six Christmas concert,' he adds, tapping his chest indignantly. '*The Snowman*. Not a dry eye.'

'*We're trumping in the air . . .*' trills Darren launching into a constipated snowman routine.

Kev dives at Darren, wrapping his arm around his neck, half strangling him so he gurgles down to earth with a bump.

'I think you'll find it's very hard to maintain a melody when you've been told by this moron to scream,' says Kev through gritted teeth.

'OK, sorry! Keep your frillies on,' protests Darren, as Kev slowly releases his grip and recovers his dignity.

'So what *are* we going to do?' asks Ryan.

'What about your dad?' Kev suggests.

'Oh no . . . No. I am *not* having my dad play in the band!' says Ryan. 'You'll want my auntie Joan in next.'

'Can she play something?'

'Darren! We are supposed to be playing in front of fifty people at Ben Dalton's party in less than two hours' time. We are going to be laughed off that stage.'

'Might not be that bad.'

'What part of "laughed off the stage" is good?' asks Ryan.

'OK. Why don't we just tell him we can't play because . . . because we're all ill?' asks Kev.

'What with – terminal rickets?' Ryan retorts. 'Let's face it we're dead already.' He turns and looks at me thoughtfully. 'Unless . . .' he says tentatively.

I know exactly what he's going to ask and slowly shake my head. No way am I getting roped into playing in their band. Ryan gives a resigned sigh.

'At least come and watch us rehearse then.'

We go down to the little garage at the end of the garden. Inside there's a drum kit with *The Damage* painted on the biggest drum in peeling black paint, a couple of microphones on stands and some amplifiers and other kit all set up. The twins, Bruno and I make ourselves comfortable on some musty cushions at the back as Ryan, Darren and Kev get ready for their first number.

'One! Two! Three! Four!'

I don't think anything could have prepared me for what happens next.

The noise is horrible. Truly awful. I think of poor Mrs Woollacott next door and wonder how she hasn't sent her Steven round long ago.

Harry and Tom cover their ears and within half a minute run out yelling. Bruno starts howling in sympathy but I sit tight, listening politely but longing for the moment when it's all going to stop. To be fair, Ryan on the drums isn't bad and if Kev didn't scream instead of sing it might be bearable.

Finally it does stop. The silence is deafening. Ryan looks at me.

'Dad's got an old violin upstairs. Used to play in a folk band before Mum . . . How about I just . . . well, just go and get it?'

And he looks at me with such desperation my resolve crumbles. I think how he saved Bruno today and how much I want him not to look like a numpty in front of fifty of his school mates, and before I know it I'm nodding my head.

Chapter 27

Ellie

When I get back to the caravan, Grace and Bruno aren't home yet so I decide to write a bit more of my story, but the words won't flow and just as I'm getting to the bit where the evil fairy steals the human baby from its cot then substitutes her own child, the door opens and Bruno bounds in followed by Grace. I give him a quick pat on the head and carry on writing.

'You OK?' Grace asks me, opening a tin of dog food for Bruno, who watches her hungrily.

'Course.'

But Grace being Grace knows that I'm not.

'Mum wouldn't mind if you bring your friends back here. It's not like Dad's around.'

'Don't want them here,' I say as casually as I can.

'Because of me?' Grace asks.

'No.'

'What's the matter?'

'Nothing.'

'Have you fallen out with them?'

'No. Why should I?'

I avoid her eye, ashamed of how I pretended today that she wasn't my sister.

'Look, Ellie, I know they don't like me, but you don't have to stick up for me or anything.'

I can feel tears pricking at the backs of my eyes.

'What have they said to you?' she asks.

I wipe my face with my palms and glance out of the window to see Ryan waiting.

'Nothing. Go off with your boyfriend.'

'He's not my boyfriend,' she insists. 'He's just . . . a friend.'

'Whatever,' I retort gruffly, bending my head over the exercise book in front of me.

She heads for the door.

'I'll be back in a couple of hours. Will you be OK on your own till then?'

'I'm thirteen. I'm not a little kid!'

'I know.'

I look up. 'Grace?'

'Yeah?'

'I'm sorry.'

'Don't be daft!' she tells me. 'You've got nothing to be sorry for.'

But I had and I was.

I watch them disappear down the field, with Ryan happily chatting to Grace who nods and smiles every now and then. Half an hour later, I brush my hair and pull on my jacket. Bruno looks up hopefully, thinking I'm going to be taking him for another walk.

'Be good,' I tell him, 'I'll be back soon.'

I find the scrap of paper where Cait has scribbled down the address of the party, telling myself I'll only stay for half an hour so I'll be back long before Grace or Mum return. They won't even know that I've gone.

I never got invited to parties at home. I used to feel so jealous when I overheard the other girls at school talking about going to so and so's and what an amazing time they all had. I did have my own party once, when I was eight. I'd been excited for weeks and finally the day arrived, I put on my brand new dress and felt like a princess.

Everything was perfect: the sitting room was decorated with fairy lights and balloons, and Dad did a magic show. I was so proud of him and happy and everyone said it was the best party ever.

Then at teatime, disaster struck. I dropped a huge piece of gooey birthday cake, *splat* onto my new dress. I tried to scrape it all off before Dad saw, but in my panic I made things worse as the thick chocolate icing stuck like brown sludge.

I could hear Dad about to come in so I whispered to Grace not to tell and covered my dress as best as I could with a paper serviette, hoping he wouldn't notice.

But of course he did. He whipped the serviette off my lap and told everyone I was the most revolting and messiest child in the world and that I should wear a bib all the time. He kept going on and on. Then he tied a huge towel around my neck and said, 'That's better!' as everyone roared with laughter.

I ran to the bathroom, pulled off the towel and sat on the floor, listening while the party carried on without me. When I was sure everyone had gone home, I crept downstairs but all the fairy lights and balloons had vanished and there was no trace that it had ever been my birthday. From then on I never wanted another party and never got invitations to other people's.

But tonight is going to be different, I tell myself. Tonight I'm going to have a wonderful time.

I find my way to the community hall in the square, and see Cait being dropped off by her dad.

'Hey,' I call. 'Wait for me!'

'You made it!' she says happily, running over and hugging me delicately.

'You look amazing!' I tell her. And she does. Her dress looks really glamorous and expensive and she's wearing high-heeled shoes and carrying a little matching bag and her hair is beautifully curled and piled up on top.

'Dressed to impress!' she tells me, craning her head around the door looking for someone.

'Can you see Abs?' I ask.

'She can't come, has to go to her auntie's. She was really mad,' she says, hooking her arm through mine. 'Never mind. You're much more fun. Come on.'

Cait pulls me inside and we weave our way down to the front of the hall. We mess about giggling as we dance silly dances to the music, although from time to time I notice that she's still looking around for someone. I spot PJ talking and laughing with his bunch of mates, and after a while he comes over.

'You could have made a bit of an effort,' he tells Cait.

'Get lost PJ,' she replies.

'So what's your little friend's name then?' he asks, looking me up and down. He does that cute lopsided grin thing and suddenly I feel butterflies fluttering around my stomach.

'Elle, Elle Smith,' I say, tucking a strand of hair behind my ear and beaming back at him.

'So, Elle-Elle Smith,' he says with a straight face, 'dipped your head in a vat of Tango, did you?'

It takes a second to register what he's just said as the butterflies explode inside my stomach.

I'm about to say something not very polite when to my astonishment, Grace walks onto the stage with Ryan and two other boys. My mouth drops open as the audience cheers, claps and whistles.

As Grace tucks her violin under her chin she suddenly spots me, registers her surprise then gives a tiny wave.

'Let's face it, Elle, you're not as hot as your sister, are you?' PJ says, nodding at Grace.

'Sister?' asks Cait, looking from Grace to me.

'Yeah – old Frosty Pants on the fiddle,' he says. 'The Girl Without A Voice.'

Cait turns to me. 'She's your *sister*?'

For a split second I hesitate but then I take a deep breath and say clearly and loudly, 'Yeah, that's my sister – Grace.' I turn to PJ. 'And don't ever call her names again.'

PJ sniggers. 'Whoooaaa! You're scaring me, Titch.'

How could I ever have thought for one tiny moment that I liked this boy?

'Hang on,' says Cait, 'you told me you didn't know her!'

'Only because you fancy Ryan,' I blurt out.

PJ explodes into sniggers and Cait's face turns red with anger.

'I do not!' she protests furiously.

'You do – you're always going on about him. I can't help it if he likes Grace better.'

'Well, you can forget hanging around with me and my friends from now on!' Cait retorts angrily.

'Fine!' I snap back. 'I don't care.' But even as I glare angrily at her, a little voice inside me is telling me that I do care. I really do.

'Yeah and I don't give a monkey's if your dad's some fancy actor, and your mum's a la-di-da author. You're finished, Elle.'

'That's what you think. You don't know me one little bit.'

'Fiiiiiight!' calls PJ, relishing the drama.

But Cait isn't listening. She swivels round on her high heels and swishes off.

'Go on, Titch, thump her one!'

'Drop dead!' I tell him.

I'm filled with anger and about to run off too, but everyone crowds up towards the stage to listen to the band, so I'm hemmed in and can't move. The band starts to play, and I'm forced to slowly calm down. As I listen, I realise that with Grace on violin, they're amazing. I watch as Ryan grins at her happily the whole time and the other two lads look like they've died and gone to heaven – until the bass guitarist gets a bit excited and accidentally topples off the stage. But the audience don't care. They think it's just part of the act and cheer him as he climbs back on, so he does it again and again, just for effect.

They play non-stop for three-quarters of an hour, by which time all my anger has drained away and everyone's dancing; even the bald caretaker is head-banging away, flicking his imaginary tresses to and fro.

Finally they stop, Ryan yells, 'Thank you and goodnight!' and they run off stage like pop stars. Everyone calls for an encore and I can hear people asking who 'that girl' was. And at the back of the hall I spot Cait leaning against the wall with her arms folded and a scowl on her face. PJ sidles up next to her and slides his arm around her waist but she doesn't push him away.

And although I know I've done the right thing and I'm glad that I said what I said, and I'm not even angry any more, I still feel sad and flat, like all the fairy lights have vanished and the balloons have popped and all I want to do is to go back to the caravan, right now.

Chapter 28

Grace

Ryan walks us home. Ellie's completely quiet but as he's never met her before, I think he just assumes she's like me so he talks for the three of us. He's bursting with enthusiasm and tries to convince me I should play in the band again. He says we could even audition for 'Beachfest', some big music festival taking place next month. Up till now he hasn't dared put The Damage down but with me playing, he says they'd stand a really good chance of getting picked.

We take the shortcut down the path through the stones, something I'd never dream of doing after dark if I was on my own or just with Ellie, but with Ryan walking between us I feel safe.

The moon comes out from behind the clouds and suddenly the stones are bathed in its clear pale light. There's a faint white mist rising from the ground like soft breath, blurring the edges of each stone. For a brief moment I imagine the group of young girls, magically released from their stone prisons, dazed by their unexpected transformation back to their human form.

We reach the caravan and thankfully Mum isn't back from

the fishermen's meal at the café yet. Ellie rushes straight in. I know there's something wrong because back at the community hall she didn't say a word when I told her we should be getting home. I thought she'd kick up a fuss as it was so early but she just hurried off to collect her jacket as if she couldn't wait to leave. She didn't even say goodbye to her friend.

'Grace,' Ryan says, as I'm about to follow Ellie into the caravan. I stop and turn around. He's holding out a scrap of paper. Puzzled, I take it.

'I meant to give you this earlier. One of the twins found it in the kitchen. It must have fallen out of your jumper pocket.'

I stare at the folded paper blankly, then realise to my horror it's my list about him. I prickle with embarrassment. Please, don't let him have read it, I pray silently. Please! I put my hand to my face but he guesses my thoughts.

'I'd be lying if I told you I didn't read it. Harry insisted it was mine because he'd seen my name at the top. I just wanted to put the record straight.'

Mortified, I unfold the paper and realise that next to my stupid list there's more writing, in black felt pen.

Ryan

You're funny.
Only cos I want to make you smile.

You stuck up for me.
Someone has to stand up to the old rottweiler.

You're thoughtful.
Can't help looking blank. You're on my mind all the time.

Kind.

An incurable character defect obliges me to help the following:

- small furry animals

- kid brothers (I keep putting them on eBay but no takers)

- random old ladies across the road, whether they want to or not.

I am urgently seeking therapy.

Pretty smart.

Wrong boy.

But are you for real?

Yes I am, so you don't ever need to be afraid of me.

'I'm not afraid of you one little bit!' a voice says, out of the blue. 'I love being with you.'

We stare at each other in shock as I realise that voice was mine. Ryan hadn't expected me to say anything. But then nor had I. The words just fell out of my mouth, easy as breathing. Ryan tries to speak but now he's the one tongue-tied – completely lost for words.

Finally he takes a gulp of air, shrugs, grins and diving forward, gently kisses my cheek. Then he turns and runs full pelt back down the field towards the beach. Ellie appears in the caravan doorway.

'Think he likes you . . . or what?' she says, rolling her eyes.

'Think I like him too.' I reply quietly.

'Grace Smith, what is *happening* to you?' she asks in surprise.

I shiver inside. 'I'm waking up.'

And suddenly I imagine I'm one of those Maids, brought

back to life, free to breathe and move and dance once again.

'Cracking up, more like,' Ellie retorts. 'But I suppose you were pretty good tonight. Let's face it, if it wasn't for you, they would have been seriously average.'

'So you think I should join the band?' I ask her.

She gives a little shrug.

'What's the matter, Ellie?' I ask.

'Nothing,' she says with a big false smile. 'I'm deliriously happy.'

'You can tell me.'

'No, I can't. But Gracie, although everything's rubbish, it's all sorted. OK?'

'I guess that's all right then,' I reply confused.

I lose sight of Ryan in the darkness but seconds later hear a faint but joyous whoop from the beach and know that it's him. I grip the note tightly and follow Ellie inside, smiling all over and feeling like my whole world has suddenly flipped upside down.

Chapter 29

Ellie

I'm dreading going into school today because I'll have to face Cait, Abs and all the other girls. But then, I think sadly, maybe I won't actually have to face them; they'll just give me the cold shoulder and I'll be on my own again, like I used to be at my last school. I try not to think about this as I walk, head down, into my form room.

Abs, Ruby, Shareen and Freya come rushing up to me. My heart beats faster – are they going to have a go at me? That would probably be worse than being ignored.

'You've got it!' Ruby shrieks as Shareen and Freya both try to hug me.

I look at them blankly.

'Mad Mulligan's chosen you!' squeals Shareen excitedly.

'What for?'

'Princess Caraboo, what else?' says Abs.

'But . . . what about Cait?' I ask, my mind spinning in excitement as I dare for a moment to think of myself playing the lead role.

'Oh, she's Lady of the Manor,' Freya tells me.

'But —'

'It's fine, Elle. So what if someone else gets to be the star – for a change,' adds Freya with just a hint of cattiness in her voice. 'Anyway, you were *loads* better than her.'

My heart's beating excitedly. 'Did you really think so?' I ask.

'Definitely. You're a natural.'

'Am I?'

'Yeah,' says Ruby. 'You were totally brilliant.'

I'm glowing inside. More of the class crowd round, everyone's looking at me and saying how great I am and I feel like I'm on top of the world.

'I reckon you'll end up an actor like your dad,' Shareen says.

The mention of Dad brings me suddenly back down to earth with a bump.

'Doubt it,' I mumble, guiltily.

'Let's face it. All your family's talented,' says Ruby. 'Daisy Millar told me that the new girl in Ryan's band is your sister!'

'No wonder you didn't want to tell Cait about her!' says Abs with a gasp.

'Yeah, I'd have kept that quiet too,' adds Freya with a snort of a giggle. 'Cait's fancied him for years.'

'So is Ryan going out with her or are they just in the band together?'

'Um . . . I don't know.'

'Cait's not going to like it, whatever,' says Ruby.

'Oh give over, Ruby! Who cares what she likes? Why should she be the centre of attention all the time?' asks Freya. 'Well, I think your sister's amazing. Ryan's band used to be rubbish.'

'Even though *he's* totally gorgeous, of course!' says Shareen with a lovestruck sigh.

There's a sudden awkward silence as Cait walks into the room.

'Hi,' says Abs.

'Elle's going to be Princess Caraboo,' calls Freya.

Cait pastes a smile on her face. 'Really,' she says, flicking her long brown hair over her shoulder as if she didn't care one bit. 'You'll be great.'

'Thanks.'

I smile back at her but there's a thin, but very solid, icy wall between us now. Abs and Freya notice immediately and looks dart between them, but neither of them says anything out loud, even though at least twice in the next few minutes Cait glances sideways at me, as if she's sizing me up.

She doesn't sit next to me in French like she usually does, but hangs back in the corridor talking to PJ. Both Shareen and Freya rush over to fill the empty seat next to me. Freya wins but promises Shareen she'll let her sit next to me in double art. Cait glances over at us as PJ is telling her to 'park her fat bum' on a bench outside the dining hall at breaktime and wait there for him. Instead of giving him a mouthful like I expect her to, she doesn't say a word – she just nods.

Chapter 30

Grace

I didn't think anything would be different at school today but from the minute I walk into class it seems I've stumbled into a parallel universe.

'You were amazing!' Daisy Millar gushes, looking at me for the first time as if I haven't crawled out from under a stone.

'I've asked my Mum to book The Damage for my party, but only if you're playing,' says her friend Amy. 'You will be, won't you?'

From the other side of the classroom, I spot Ryan watching me. I nod and smile at Amy as a huge, relieved grin sweeps over his face, and I feel a strange but delicious fluttery feeling in my stomach.

'Yesss!' he shouts just as Miss Turner enters the room. 'Yes! Yes! Yes! Oh yes!'

'Ryan, stop jigging about like a moron,' she orders cheerfully.

'Yes, Miss Turner! Straight away, Miss Turner!'

'Baxter, have you been sniffing something?'

'No. Just happy, Miss Turner.'

'How extremely thrilling for you. And would this have anything to do with your performance at the community hall on Saturday night?'

'They were sooo cool, Miss!' one of the girls calls out.

'Curb your enthusiasm, Kaylee. It's frighteningly unnatural.'

'But you should have heard them.'

'I live two doors down from the hall. I could hardly avoid it.'

'So what do you think, Miss? Wicked or what?'

'Well, I have to admit I was, in fact, pleasantly shocked. Instead of the usual cat-strangling cacophony that Ryan and his entourage have honed to perfection, I heard . . . I heard . . . music.'

'That was Grace on violin.'

'Really! Well, Miss Smith, I shall inform Mr Brightwell, and no doubt he will recruit you into our magnificent school orchestra where your considerable talents can be put to more productive use.'

I stare at her in alarm but then catch Ryan smiling at me and relax, realising I don't care if they make me play in the orchestra or not. It might even be fun.

To my delight, Miss Turner moves straight on to form business and completely ignores me for the rest of the registration session. Ryan and I head off to our first lesson and I find myself speaking to him – OK, quietly, and only when there's no one else around – but I speak! We talk. Our conversation is slow at first, tentative, awkward even. We bat words clumsily to and fro like two kids playing ping-pong for the first time. We're both as nervous as each other. But soon it becomes easier, and although I don't say a word about Dad, after a while it's as if we're old friends meeting for the first time in years. And I'm the happiest I've ever been.

At lunchtime I'm in the cloakroom when Ellie rushes up.

'Grace, Grace, guess what?' she says urgently.

'What's wrong?' I ask, eyeing her nervously.

'I'm Princess Caraboo!'

'What?'

'The school play! I auditioned. I'm the lead, Princess Caraboo! First rehearsal in five minutes!' she tells me excitedly.

'That's fantastic!' I say.

'And there's another rehearsal after school tonight so don't wait for me, I'll meet you back home.'

'Um . . . I . . . might go to Ryan's first – but I'll be home before Mum gets back,' I reply, wondering what she'll say.

'Oh, OK.'

I needn't have worried, she's far too excited about the play to digest anything I've just said.

'And well done you,' I add. 'Break a leg or something . . .'

She turns to go and I see her friend Cait staring at us both. She's sitting with PJ who's whispering in her ear. I expect her to say something or join Ellie as she walks past but to my surprise, she completely ignores her.

When Cait does get up to go, PJ tries to hold on to her, but she gives a little laugh, breaks free then hurries down the corridor towards the school hall. PJ glances over at me.

'All right, Frosty?' he asks. 'Changed your mind about going out with me? Just say the word.'

I turn away and hurry off.

Chapter 31

Ellie

I quickly discover Mad Mulligan isn't quite as bonkers as she first seemed, but she still works us like a maniac on a mission.

'OK, everyone, listen up,' she bellows, reducing the room to silence. 'You've got just a few short weeks until your first performance. There'll be rehearsals most days after school. I want all lines learnt by next Monday. No excuses. If you're not happy, leave *right* now and don't waste my time!' She points melodramatically to the door as if hordes of us were going to suddenly stampede out. Nobody moves.

'Right. You may all have the brains and bodies of sensitive young adolescents but while you're in this hall you're going to be professional actors . . . because when your big night finally comes and you get up on that stage and act your little hearts out – I want the audience to adore you, to worship you . . . not to snigger into their boots. OK. Let's do this.'

For the next three-quarters of an hour we work our socks off as Mulligan stamps and shouts and orders us about like the biggest diva this side of the western world.

I'm dreading all the scenes I share with Cait. Word is going round that we've had a bust up and aren't talking. But as I get into the part, forgetting I'm just Ellie Smith acting like a drama queen in some school play, the tension builds between us and by the climax of our big scene when the Lady of the Manor accuses Princess Caraboo of being a fraud and she's fighting back with all the energy she can muster, the atmosphere in the room is electric and I suddenly realise I'm physically shaking. At the end, everyone breaks out into spontaneous applause and even Mad Mulligan is raving.

'That was amazing, girls! Fantastic! Elle you really nailed that scene,' she tells us as if we were on some TV talent show or something. 'You keep it up and this play is going to be the best this school has ever produced. If it's that good, we'll take it to the drama festival next term. And come back with a stonking big trophy!'

As I glow in her praise, I notice the look on Cait's face and the light in her eyes. We may not be friends any more, I think bitterly, but being enemies has some benefits.

I'm loving every single moment I'm on stage and I'm devastated when the rehearsal finishes all too quickly. Once Mad Mulligan calls time and tells us to hurry back to our lessons, Cait looks through me as if I am invisible. She walks straight past me, waving to PJ who's standing at the hall doorway, waiting for her.

'You were total dog poo!' he announces loudly, so everyone can hear.

Her face flushes red and she stares at him, embarrassed.

'Only joking!' he says as he hugs her, but the look on his face says different and I realise that he's enjoying seeing her squirm.

For one tiny moment he reminds me of Dad.

They walk off up the corridor, with his arm clamped around her shoulder, pulling her tightly towards him, and suddenly I feel I should say something, call out, warn her. But we're not friends any more – we officially hate each other. So I don't. I don't say a word. Besides, what could I say? *Be careful, Cait, PJ is like my dad?*

I haven't actually told her or anyone else what my dad is really like and I would never dream of doing that, so she wouldn't have a clue what I was talking about.

She's late into registration but makes an excuse about having to see one of the teachers. As she slips past me to the desk in front of mine she leans over and coldly whispers one word.

'Liar.'

Chapter 32

Grace

I catch Ellie after school as she's hurrying down to the hall for her second play rehearsal.

'How's it going?' I ask.

'Great,' she tells me as she darts a wary glance at Cait, a few metres ahead of her.

'Want me to hang around?' I ask, trying to disguise my concerned big sister voice.

'Give over,' she retorts. 'See you back home.'

She runs into the hall. A couple of girls rush up to her and the three of them start to chatter excitedly together. Cait hangs back, leaning on the other side of the stage, staring at Ellie with daggers drawn and I'm wondering what's going on between them as Ryan approaches.

'You ready?' he asks.

I nod. 'Let's go,' I whisper, glancing at Ellie who's totally forgotten I'm here as she giggles with her friends.

As we walk back to Ryan's house, he tells me more about Beachfest.

'There'll be fireworks and about eight bands. Maybe even a

big name or two. It's on every year, in aid of the lifeboat station down on the quay,' he says. 'Dad used to be a crew member.'

He's quiet for a moment.

'He saved a man from drowning once,' he adds quietly.

'Is . . . is that why he's in a wheelchair now?' I ask.

'No.' Ryan replies, his face clouding. 'He's ill. He's got MS.'

I look at him blankly.

'It's a horrible illness that creeps up on you, slowly paralysing you, till you can't move.'

'That's awful, Ryan, I'm so sorry.'

'Yeah, well, it's very slow, and sometimes he even seems to get a bit better for a little while, and there's always new cures, aren't there? Stem cells . . . I dunno, stuff like that, so it's not all doom and gloom. I'm sorry I . . . it's just I want to do something – something to make him proud of me, and the band's all I can think of.'

'Ryan, he is already proud of you,' I tell him, squeezing his arm gently. 'But I promise I'll play this gig if we get through the audition.'

'Thanks, Grace, it means the world to me . . . The auditions start next week so we'll have a bit of time to rehearse.'

As we turn into his road we see his dad driving along the pavement ahead of us, in his motorised wheelchair with the twins dressed in their school uniforms holding their book bags, seated but wriggling on his lap. One of the twins turns and sees us and Ryan's dad gives a couple of toots on the horn attached to the handlebars. The twins jump off at the gate and rush to put down a little ramp at the front door. Their dad manoeuvres the chair up the path, past the tangle of bikes and go-carts and bodyboards, then glides smoothly through the front door.

'Hi, Grace! Always nice to see you!' he calls.

'Hello, Mr Baxter,' I say, finding my voice.

'Well, come on in then,' he calls. 'Let's get that kettle on, Ryan my man.'

We go inside and he makes tea for us while Ryan and I make a gigantic pile of marmite toast for the twins, who are starving. Once all the toast is demolished and the mugs of tea are drunk, Ryan's dad asks us to take Harry and Tom down to the beach for a while. Both the little boys insist on holding the football and a minor punch up is only just avoided when Ryan suggests I look after the ball for them.

We get to the beach and to my horror I'm pitched with the twins against Ryan.

'But I don't know how to play football!' I say.

'Don't worry,' Ryan whispers. 'It won't matter.'

And it doesn't. We chase the ball and bundle and roll about on the sand like a bunch of scrapping puppies. I'm lying down laughing so much that when Harry sits on my feet, I can't get up.

'You can be our sister, if you like,' he tells me shyly. 'Or . . . you can be our mum.'

'She's not old enough to be our mum, stupid,' Tom says. 'Anyway, if our real mum comes back we'll have two mums and nobody has two mums, do they?'

'She's not coming back,' says Harry fiercely.

'She might.'

'She's not. She said so.'

'OK, who's hungry?' Ryan interrupts, darting me a glance.

'I am!' the twins chorus.

'Last one home's a beached whale!' he shouts and we all start running full pelt along the sand. The twins are laughing now and Ryan's chasing them and roaring away, pretending to be a sea monster, and I realise for the first time ever that I'm not the only one in this world who keeps silent.

Chapter 33

Ellie

With Cait's taunt of 'liar' ringing in my ears, I'm feeling really uneasy when I go into the hall after school for rehearsals. I pretend to everyone there's nothing the matter but I can feel her watching me and when I get up on stage, I start stuttering and stumbling over my lines. I'm finding it hard to look her in the eye as I wonder nervously what she's found out.

Mad Mulligan stops us mid-scene and asks me in a disappointed voice what on earth the matter is.

'Nothing, Miss,' I say, darting a glance at Cait.

But seeing the smug expression plastered over her face works better than anything to kick me back into shape. Suddenly I'm all stirred up. There's no way I'm going to let her get to me, I think defiantly. She's not going to ruin the best thing that's ever happened in my life.

'Can we just try this scene again?' I ask.

'I think we'd better,' Mulligan says. 'And for goodness' sake, let's have the Princess Caraboo we saw in the first rehearsal, can we, please?'

'Yes, Miss.'

I act the scene afresh, as if my life depended on it. After a couple of lines, I'm no longer afraid and there's an energy inside me that I can hardly contain.

'Much better, Elle! Brilliant!' Mulligan calls to me at the end.

I breathe a secret sigh of relief as I realise I don't need to worry. No one can stop me. Not Cait, not anyone.

Mad Mulligan puts us through our paces for nearly two hours and by the time the cleaner appears, rattling the mop in her bucket and wanting to lock up, we've worked our way through the entire play. We should all be totally wrecked but there's a buzz in the room – everyone's running on adrenalin and chattering excitedly. Mulligan shouts a reminder about getting all lines learnt by next week and threatens us with a fate worse than death if we fail. Everyone is raring to go and making plans to meet up and practise lines and scenes together. Everyone that is, except Cait and me. For a moment she looks as if she wants to speak to me, but I don't hang around, and rush off quickly.

I'm walking home back along the path by the stones when I hear a voice call out. I turn around and see Cait marching towards me. It's too late to run away – I stand my ground.

Cait stares at me for a second, then says deliberately, 'You're a big fat liar, Elle, aren't you?'

'What d'you mean?' I ask nervously, playing for time.

'You said you were moving into that big house on the downs. But you're not, are you? I know for definite you're not. PJ lives on that road and he's told me another family's already moved in.'

I think fast. 'Dad put an offer in but someone must have beaten it.'

'I bet.' She stares at me. 'So what else are you making up?' she asks nastily.

'Nothing . . .'

'I don't believe you. I'm going to tell everyone what a great big liar you are. Let's see what Abs and the others think of you then!'

My heart is thumping as I scan Cait's face. She means every word.

'No one's going to think you're so brilliant, are they? Not when they know the truth about you.'

Ahead of me I see Susan. She waves. My heart sinks.

'I've got to go.'

'Ooo, Mummy going to be cross, is she?' Cait teases, eyeing Susan coldly. A smug smile sweeps across her face. 'She doesn't look a bit like a writer. More lies, Elle?'

I'm dying quietly inside as Cait marches straight up to Susan.

'Are you a writer or what?' she demands rudely.

'Um . . . Yes . . . I am actually,' Susan replies looking slightly disconcerted.

Cait looks surprised and hesitates for a second before adding, 'You really write *proper* books?'

'Well . . . I'd like to think they were proper. They get published, if that's what you mean.' She glances at me then back to Cait. 'You two friends?'

'No way!' Cait snaps before turning tail and heading off.

'Sorry about that,' I say to Susan, shivering at my narrow escape.

'Not your fault,' she says, eyeing me curiously for a second. 'How's your story going?' she asks casually.

'OK,' I lie. 'But it's only a fairy story . . . and they're just for kids.'

'I don't know about that! Most fairy stories are completely terrifying when you analyse them.' She looks at me then adds meaningfully, 'They're often about standing up to someone frightening – just like in real life.'

I know she means Cait but suddenly I'm not thinking about her, I'm thinking of Dad and how he used to bully Mum, Grace and me.

'I've got to go,' I say, feeling uncomfortable.

'OK. But if you ever want to chat about anything – stories,

friends, whatever – you know where I am.'

'Thanks,' I say quickly before turning and running all the way home. Stories and real life are completely different things, I think, and if you mix them up together, like I have, you get a whole mess of trouble. But it's too late for me to separate them out now and tell the truth. I'm in too deep.

Chapter 34

Grace

I get home five minutes before Ellie.

'How did it go?' I ask. She looks at me blankly. 'The rehearsal,' I say.

'Oh that. Well . . . it started off complete pants, then got miles better and by the time we finished it was totally brilliant. Dad was sooo right when he called me a drama queen – I'm the biggest drama queen in the whole universe!'

She stretches out her arms, twirls around the caravan, and promptly bangs into the little table.

'Ow! That hurt!' she says, rubbing her hip.

'So is your friend Cait in the play?' I ask casually.

'Why does everyone think she's my friend?' says Ellie scornfully.

'You were best mates, last week.'

'In your dreams!' she retorts, turning away to get some bread out of the fridge. 'Thought I was the one with the crazy imagination.'

'Is it because she's going out with PJ?'

'No! In fact, I'm deliriously happy for them both. They're

made for each other. Fancy a cheese and jam sandwich?'

She tilts her head back, sticks out her jaw and I know for sure she's miffed about something. Secretly I'm relieved Ellie's not the one involved with PJ, but I don't tell her that. I change the subject and as we make sandwiches together, I tell her about Ryan's family and how I'm determined to audition with the band for Beachfest.

'You'll knock'em dead.'

'Hope not, that's Darren's job when he leaps off the stage,' I say with a giggle. 'Ryan told me it's thanks to him the band got its name. After every rehearsal, when he checked out his garage, Ryan's dad would ask, "So what's the damage this time?" because Darren was always breaking something.'

We make ourselves comfy on the bench seat and munch our sarnies.

'See this pink stripy material?' asks Ellie with a mouthful of sandwich, pointing to a square on the quilt. 'Gran made Mum and Auntie Anna matching dresses for some concert they sang in. They must have looked like twins.'

'Don't get any ideas,' I joke.

'It's a shame they never used to see each other much,' Ellie says, her face suddenly serious. 'They're sisters for goodness' sake.'

'They had a big row,' I tell her quietly.

Ellie's surprised. 'I thought it was because Dad told Mum he didn't want her seeing Auntie Anna.'

'Well, he did, but I heard them both about two years ago. They didn't know I was round the side of the house with Bruno. Auntie Anna was telling Mum she shouldn't let Dad control her like he did but Mum said things were complicated and she shouldn't interfere. After a few minutes, they started arguing, then Anna got cross and stormed off.'

'That's awful,' Ellie says pulling a face. She's quiet for a few seconds. 'We'd never fall out like that, would we, Grace? I mean . . . no matter what happened.'

'Course we wouldn't,' I tell her. 'Come on, let's go and meet Mum.'

We put Bruno's lead on and head up to the café on the beach.

'She's late. She's supposed to finish at five,' Ellie says.

'She's probably just cooking up loads of pasties or something.'

'Oh let them be cheese and onion, pleeeeease!' says Ellie, clamping her palms together and pretending to pray.

When we get to the café all the blinds are pulled down.

'Looks like she's gone,' says Ellie, rushing up the wooden steps.

We burst into the café. The place has been transformed. It's festooned with twinkling white fairy lights and in the middle of the room is just one table, laid for two with a clean white linen cloth, shiny silver cutlery and bone china plates. In the centre of the table stands a tall vase full of fresh flowers.

'Where's Mum?' Ellie asks, eyeing Bill who's hovering by one of the café windows. Instead of his normal scruffy fishing gear he's wearing a stripy apron over a suit and tie. He nods over to the kitchen as Mum appears from behind the counter.

'What d'you think?' she asks, her eyes shining.

'What's going on?' Ellie asks.

'It's a surprise – for Daphne. She came out of hospital yesterday. I found out it was their fiftieth wedding anniversary last week, and Stan wanted to do something special but he didn't know what, so . . .'

'All your mum's idea,' Bill says grinning.

'They're here! Quick!' says Mum suddenly.

Like little children we all make a dash for hiding places as the café door creaks open.

Chapter 35

Ellie

I can't resist peering over the counter, even though Mum is tugging at my top.

'Get down, Ellie!' she whispers.

I do as she says even though I'm desperate to see Daphne. What would she look like? How weird would she be?

'Oh Stanley!' says a woman's voice. 'It's beautiful!' This must be her. But her voice is light and fluttery, not hard and gruff like I'm expecting.

'Blimey O'Reilly . . .' I hear Stan mutter.

'Happy anniversary!' chorus Mum and Bill, as we all emerge from our hiding places. I'm expecting to see a rough-looking woman dressed in sacking with a rope belt and a mad look in her eye, but I see a fragile old lady wearing a purple woollen suit, with her silver hair coiled up on the back of her head.

'She looks like an elderly Audrey Hepburn,' Grace whispers to me, but I haven't a clue who she means.

Daphne smiles at Mum. 'You must be Karin,' she says warmly.

'Hello,' Mum replies. 'I hope you don't mind. I thought . . . well, I just thought . . . fifty years is an awfully long time . . .'

'Thank you, my dear. You're very sweet.' She gives Mum a delicate hug. 'Fifty precious years . . . and all thanks to the Maids, eh, Stanley?' she adds, smiling at Stan.

'The Maids?' I ask, wondering if she really is bonkers after all. 'What d'you mean?'

'Just over fifty years ago, one August night, Stan and I were walking back together from a dance, but we'd had a furious argument—'

'She never wanted to see me again – ever,' Stan interrupts.

'Then just as we walked into the stone circle, the sky opened and hailstones pelted down—'

'The size of peas, the little blighters!' Stan says. 'Fired straight onto us.'

'So we ran for shelter, the only shelter nearby – this wooden hut, which wasn't a café then. It was such a wreck inside—'

'And chock full of mice and rats too, but as we weren't talking, I didn't tell Daffy that.'

'Just as well. Anyway, as we stood here shivering, ignoring each other—'

'The floor gave way and we fell onto the sand down there,' adds Stan with a chuckle, pointing to the middle of the room.

'And suddenly we were both laughing and I knew we were supposed to be together no matter what happened. Good or bad.'

'We got hitched, bought this place and turned it into the best little café for miles around.'

She reaches for Stan's hand and holds it tightly. 'And now he won't sell up, will you? You're a daft old fool,' she tells him, 'but I wouldn't have it any other way.'

With a big cough and a little flourish, Bill shows Stan and Daphne to their seats. Mum calls Grace and I over and we help carry the dishes of food to the table. Mum's certainly been busy. There's fresh grilled fish that Bill has somehow managed to catch this morning, hot fried potatoes, salads and a beautifully

146

decorated cake with golden writing, saying *Happy 50th Anniversary* on its smoothly iced surface. As we help Mum and play at waitressing, I watch Stan and Daphne chatting and laughing together and realise some stories really do have a happy ever after.

Bill goes over to the battered piano in the corner and begins playing. As he thumps out a tune, Stan gets to his feet, takes Daphne's hand, guides her to a space where the pair of them start to dance. Slowly, they waltz around the room with eyes only for each other. We watch them for a few minutes, then Mum darts a glance at me. She grins mischievously, then grabs my hand and we start dancing too. Not quite as elegantly. Grace watches, trying not to laugh.

The next tune Bill plays is much faster. It's pretty manic and Bill's hit and miss piano playing technique doesn't help much, so Stan and Daphne sit this one out as Mum offers to show us all a Czech folk dance her dad taught her and Auntie Anna when they were small. I'm not sure what my grandad would have thought but pretty soon we're all laughing and giggling as Grace and I try to imitate the steps Mum demonstrates, faster and faster.

'Beats the telly, doesn't it?' Stan jokes to Daphne as they watch and clap along, until the three of us finally collapse into an exhausted heap on the floor.

A couple of hours later, Stan, Daphne and Bill head home while Mum, Grace and I set about clearing up.

'Think I might have overdone it,' Mum says, looking at all the serving dishes still half full of food.

'Shame,' I say picking up a crispy fried potato and popping it in my mouth. We take a break, sit down together and polish off the leftovers.

'What you did for Stan and Daphne was really kind, Mum,' I tell her.

She gives a little shrug and smiles. 'I enjoyed it,' she says simply. 'It's funny, but Stan seems almost like family now.'

She pulls a face and I suddenly realise how much she must miss Auntie Anna. If only there was something I could do, I think. Just like Stan and Daphne, they go back a long way. I want their story to be happy ever after too.

That night, when we get back to the caravan, I open my notebook thinking I might give my story one last try and the postcard of the stone circle falls out. As I stare at it an idea forms in my head. The Maids brought Stan and Daphne together; maybe they could work their magic on other people too. I quickly turn the card over, address it to Auntie Anna, then write a short message. I don't say much, just that Mum, Grace and I are living down here in a caravan.

The next day on our way to school, I make an excuse to Grace then dive into the little post office, buy a stamp and quickly post the card.

'What you up to?' Grace asks me as I come out.

'Nothing,' I reply.

Chapter 36

Grace

After registration, as Turner dismisses us, Ryan hurries over and tells me the Beachfest organiser rang him last night and wants the band to audition straight after school today.

'Today!' I whisper aghast. 'You said next week!'

'Don't worry, it'll be OK. If we play all the stuff we played at Ben's party we'll sail through. Then once we're in, we can spend the next few weeks rehearsing for the actual gig.'

'Where's the audition?'

'Same place. The community hall.'

'OK,' I tell him nervously, as the bell rings. 'I'll meet you there.'

For the next hour during lessons, I'm in a daze thinking about the audition. I know how important it is to Ryan and don't want to let him down. At the beginning of morning break I'm hurrying down the corridor to find Ellie to tell her what's happening, when I see Cait and PJ in the cloakroom, ahead of me.

'Hey, Frosty, your dad know Spielberg?' PJ calls.

Wondering what on earth he's talking about, I speed up

hoping to get past them both quickly, but PJ has other ideas and blocks my path.

Glancing at Cait, he jibes, 'Your little sister reckons he's some big shot actor.'

I disguise the surprise on my face and try to dodge past him but he grabs my arm and swings me round.

'I reckon he does toilet cleaner adverts,' he says with a snigger. 'Can't get paid much if you're living in some crappy caravan, can he?'

I try to jerk away my arm but he clings on tightly, smirking all the while.

'PJ, leave her,' Cait says uncomfortably, but he doesn't. He makes a grab for my other arm. But this time I'm too quick for him and using the palm of my free hand under his chin, I push his face up and away with all my strength. He loses his balance momentarily and falls back, straight onto Miss Turner.

'Jacobs!' she snaps, steadying herself, 'What on earth are you playing at?'

'It was her, Miss, she pushed me,' PJ says with a scowl, pointing at me.

Miss Turner glares at me.

'So what's the story, Miss Smith?' she demands.

I open my mouth to try to speak but no sound comes out. My palms are suddenly sweaty and I've got that awful queasy feeling. I stand, rooted to the spot, in silence. Ten seconds seem like ten hours. PJ smirks, as I stare back at Miss Turner.

'Well, say something!'

But I don't. I can't.

'Detention, this afternoon,' she snaps irritably. 'Both of you.'

PJ's face falls.

'But I'm innocent, Miss!' he pleads. 'I've been assaulted. I'm a victim.'

'Three-thirty. My office,' says Miss Turner, walking off.

150

The second she goes, I run off down the corridor.

'Hey, say something, Frosty Pants . . . I can't hear you . . .' PJ taunts, as I dive into the girls' loos and shut myself into an empty cubicle. It's smelly and full of graffiti but I don't care, I can think of only one thing – the audition, straight after school today. I can't let Ryan down, I think desperately, I just can't. But no one messes with Miss Turner. What on earth am I going to do?

Chapter 37

Ellie

'Grace? You OK?' I ask.

'No . . . yeah. . . um . . . I can't meet you after school,' she tells me as we walk down the corridor together. 'Something's come up.'

'Like what?'

'The band audition . . . and . . .' She pulls a face. '. . . detention with Miss Turner.'

'At the same time?'

She nods.

'What you going to do?' I ask horrified. I've seen Miss Turner in the dinner hall vaporising noisy pupils at ten paces, and although teachers don't usually scare me, she gives me the heeby-jeebies.

'Not sure.'

'You'll be in massive trouble if you don't go.'

She suddenly looks at me. 'Ellie, why have you told everyone that Dad's an actor?' she asks out of the blue.

'I had to say something,' I tell her. 'People were asking about him – what else could I do?'

'But an actor? In America?'

'What do you want me to say?' I snap back at her. 'You want me to tell them the truth?'

'You didn't have to lie.'

'Yes . . . I did.' I can feel the anger bubbling up inside me. 'Grace, we've got a brand new life now. We can be anyone we want. You've got Ryan, I've never seen Mum so happy – and for the first time ever . . . I've actually got friends.'

'So what happens when all these friends find out you've just spun them a story?'

'They won't. I'm not going to let anything or anyone spoil things. I don't want to be a nobody again, OK?'

'What you talking about?'

'I'm a totally different person here. I'm Elle Smith, the girl everyone thinks is great.'

'Ellie, be careful.'

'Don't tell me what to do, cos I'm not listening.'

I spin around and stride off, leaving her standing. I head out to the playground and find Abs, Ruby and Freya. From the look on their faces I guess the rumours have reached them too.

'Cait's been telling everyone you're not moving to that house on the downs,' Abs says.

I take a deep breath. 'It's true,' I tell them.

'What?' asks Freya, surprised.

'I was pretty upset last week . . . didn't want to say anything but Dad messed up and someone else got the house,' I say with a disappointed shrug. 'I suppose Cait's got it in for me now, and is telling everyone I'm a liar and I was never moving there in the first place.'

'She is.'

'Thought she might. She doesn't like me being Princess Caraboo, either.'

'She's just jealous!' says Freya.

'She's a good actress and she thought she'd get the part,' I say. 'She must really hate me now. I suppose I'll just have to get used to her spreading more tales about me.'

'Well, we won't be listening!' Ruby tells me firmly.

'What a cow!' Freya adds crossly.

'Yeah. I'm not going to ask her to my party next month,' Ruby says.

'She wouldn't come anyway,' says Abs. 'She's always hanging around with PJ now – she doesn't care about her old friends.'

'Well, that suits me fine,' says Ruby.

'Shhh, she's over there,' says Abs suddenly.

'Who cares,' says Freya. 'Let's go before she makes up something else about Elle.'

Freya links arms with me but as we all pass Cait sitting on her own, I catch her eye and remember what it was like not having friends to chat and giggle and hang out with, and suddenly I don't feel like 'Elle the girl everyone thinks is great' any more. I just feel mean and small and rotten.

Chapter 38

Grace

I walk down to Turner's office after the bell goes for the end of school, with a sick feeling in my stomach. I peer inside and spot her busily tapping away on her computer, waiting for the day's wrongdoers to troop in. I'm about to step through the doorway and sit down quietly when, to my surprise, I turn around. As if my feet and legs no longer belong to me and are moving of their own accord, I stride off back up the corridor, through the entrance, across the playground and out of the school gates. I break into a run and don't stop running until I get home.

I'm shaking as I lean underneath the back of the caravan, find the key Mum always hides inside the old metal watering can and quickly let myself in. I give Bruno a quick cuddle then collect my violin, lock up and hurry back along the path by the stones and down into town till I arrive at the community hall. I'm seriously out of breath when I see Ryan, Darren and Kev outside unloading their gear from Darren's mum's car.

'Good luck, my darling!' Darren's mum says, grabbing him enthusiastically around the neck and giving him a huge smacker of a kiss, daubing his already bright red cheeks with her lipstick.

'Gerofff!' he yells, breaking free and wiping his face as Kev sniggers away behind him.

Ryan rushes up to me. 'Ready?' he asks with an eager smile.

I nod, smiling to hide my nervousness, then help him carry everything inside.

We discover we're last on the audition list. Ryan is pleased because this means we can check out the competition, but waiting around just gives me more time to worry about Miss Turner and how angry she'll be when I don't turn up for detention.

Finally, the first band appears on stage. Thirty seconds into their performance, we exchange relieved glances and then exaggerated grimaces as we realise they're not very good at all. The second group is worse still and Kev's quietly boasting about a walkover, but then the following four bands are totally brilliant and we begin to worry that we have some serious rivals. Only three under-eighteen bands will have the chance to play at the festival, all the others being older groups or bigger names.

Finally it's our turn and we climb up on stage. The next five minutes are a complete blur. Darren keeps a low profile thanks to Ryan's earlier threat that if anyone leaps off the stage, he'll personally pull their arms and legs off, but he still manages to bounce from corner to corner like a hyperactive kangaroo. We're halfway through our song when out of the corner of my eye I notice someone walk in the back of the hall.

To my horror, I realise it's Miss Turner and immediately play a couple of wrong notes. Ryan glances over, surprised. I quickly recover and continue playing as she stands at the back, her arms folded, staring at us with that severe look on her face. All of a sudden it's hard work making my fingers play the notes I want them to. Darren is freaked too and freezes like a rabbit caught in headlights but somehow we manage to get through the rest of the song without totally falling apart.

We finish our audition and the judges start to confer in whispers while we head back to our seats to wait for the results. Miss Turner approaches us. She's folding a sheet of paper that she's been writing on.

'Bravo, Miss Smith,' she says. 'All in all, quite a performance. You will be in detention for the rest of this week to make up for the one you've missed today. Give this to your parents. I look forward to meeting them,' she adds, handing me the note.

'Uh oh,' I hear Darren mumble.' Someone's in deep —'

'Darren!' Miss Turner snaps, walking off.

'Nothing, Miss. Sorry, Miss,' Darren grovels.

Ryan looks at me. 'Thank you,' he says.

We have to wait another ten minutes before the judges make their final decision.

'OK, everyone,' calls a guy dressed completely in black and wearing sunglasses even though it's dark and gloomy in the hall, 'this is a really hard call because the talent here today is truly amazing, so some of you are going to go home disappointed. The bands we want to play at the festival this year are, Song Guild, Curly Boys and . . . The Damage.'

Ryan, Kev and Darren let out excited whoops.

'We're in!' says Ryan, hugging me tightly.

'Yeaaaaaooooo! I love you, mate!' Darren yells, leaping up and hugging the guy in black, accidentally knocking the sunglasses off his face as he reels back in alarm.

'Sorry . . .' Darren mutters. 'Bit overexcited.'

Chapter 39

Ellie

When I get back from the play rehearsal, Mum is already home but there's no sign of Grace.

'What's up?' I ask, seeing her sitting at the table.

She doesn't reply so I glance at the note lying in front of her. It's from Miss Turner, saying Grace has failed to attend a detention today; she's extremely concerned about her behaviour, and wants to see Mum or Dad as soon as possible.

'Grace only bunked off because she had an audition,' I say.

'Audition?' asks Mum, puzzled.

'She's in a band.'

'Grace?'

'Yeah. They're really good. Thanks to her.'

Mum picks up the note and stares at it. 'But what on earth has she done to be in so much trouble at school?'

'Nothing. Turner picks on her because she won't talk.'

Mum gives a long sigh.

'Why won't Grace talk to you either?' I ask. 'I mean, I can understand other people but . . . '

Mum doesn't answer for a few seconds, but pulls a face and

shakes her head.

'I let her down,' she says finally.

'How come?'

'A couple of years ago I promised her I'd speak to someone about your dad.'

'What happened?'

'I got scared. Really frightened. I realised if I said anything, you and Grace might be taken away from me. Your dad was always threatening me he'd make it happen. And more than anything else in the world I couldn't bear that. So I kept quiet. Put up with everything, hoping it might get better one day. But it didn't, it just got worse. I fell out with Anna and then Gran died – I had nowhere to go and no money and so . . . I stayed.'

Mum cups her face in her hands and I know she's crying. The door of our bedroom clicks open and Grace appears. She puts her arms around Mum and buries her face in her neck.

'I'm sorry, Grace. But to lose you and Ellie would have been the end of my world,' Mum whispers. 'I couldn't do it.'

'For goodness' sake, speak to her Grace!' I snap. 'Say something!'

Grace tries to speak but no words come out. Instead she hugs Mum tighter.

'It's all right, love,' Mum says. 'It's my fault. You trusted me. I don't blame you one bit.'

She takes a deep breath and folds up the letter.

'And don't worry about this. I'll go and see this Miss Turner tomorrow and find out what terrible things you've been up to at school.'

Grace nods and tries to smile.

'That's better. Well, she can't eat me, can she?' Mum asks.

Grace and I exchange glances. Turner would have her for breakfast with a fried egg on top.

But the next day Mum is as good as her word. She dresses in a pair of smart black trousers and a neat long-sleeved blouse, clothes she hasn't worn since she was with Dad. She brushes her hair carefully and puts on her full make-up.

'My armour,' she says with a determined expression, as she pulls on her coat. 'Don't worry, Grace, I'll sort this out. Everything's going to be all right.'

She leaves half an hour before us so she can catch Miss Turner before school starts.

When we arrive, we see her coming out of Turner's office.

Her face is pale but she still has that same determined look as she walks calmly down to the school entrance and meets us by the doorway.

'What happened?' I ask.

'Nothing. I just told her that Grace is a hard-working, conscientious student who always does her best, and that's good enough for me.' Mum takes a deep breath and I see her hands are shaking. 'And now I'm going to go home, change out of these clothes and make myself a very strong cup of tea.'

She smiles at us both and turns to go.

'Mum . . .' Grace calls after her in barely a whisper.

Stopping in her tracks, Mum slowly turns and looks at her. Grace opens her mouth but it's a good two seconds before any words come out.

'I . . . I'll see you later then,' she says finally.

Mum bites her lip, blinks back the tears filling her eyes and nods. Then she quickly hurries off, through the playground and out of the school gates, threading her way around everyone rushing in as the school bell sounds.

Chapter 40

Grace

I've wanted to speak to Mum for so long. Saying those few words was like lifting a curse on me. First Ryan, and now Mum; soon I'll be able to talk to anyone I want. I walk into registration and spot Ryan. I'm expecting him to be on a high from getting through the audition but he's sitting at a desk, his hand propped on his chin, staring out of the window. I take the seat next to him and lean over.

'What's up?' I whisper.

He shrugs.

'Nothing, everything's cool,' he mumbles.

'Are we rehearsing tonight?'

'No.'

He looks down, avoiding my eye.

'What's wrong?'

He doesn't answer. He just shakes his head slightly. I'm worried now.

'Is it your dad?'

'No, he's . . . he's OK.'

'So what's going on?'

'Nothing! Stop asking.'

Puzzled and hurt by the sharpness in his voice, and the complete change in him, I back away as Miss Turner comes in and the noise level in the room immediately dips into silence.

I glance over at Ryan throughout registration but he keeps his head down and doesn't look up once. Although Turner's as abrupt and sarcastic as ever, I notice she no longer tries to bully me into speaking. When she dismisses us, Ryan hurries out without waiting for me like he usually does.

PJ comes over.

'Dumped you then, has he?' he says with a smirk. 'Typical Ryan. Short attention span.'

I stare at him horrified. What's he talking about?

'Plenty more fish in the sea,' he adds, as I rush out of the classroom.

For the rest of the morning I tie myself up in knots thinking about Ryan and wondering what could be wrong. At lunch-break I sit on the bench where we always meet but there's no sign of him. Ellie waves to me as she comes out of the art room. She's laughing and chatting, enjoying being the centre of attention. She seems so . . . so confident now. And there's such a determined look in her eye, like she's going to be in charge, whatever.

Over the other side of the playground I spot PJ. He grins at me, and makes an exaggerated thumbs up gesture. I get up and go inside.

Chapter 41

Ellie

As I head off to rehearsals, I see Cait standing against the wall outside the hall, hanging around for PJ probably. She's been staring at me weirdly all day, right from first thing this morning in registration – a sort of knowing, smug expression, like she's waiting for just the right moment to pounce. The skin on the back of my neck prickles uncomfortably and I feel on edge. I plan on ignoring her, but as I walk past she calls after me.

'Hey, Elle . . .'

I carry on walking.

'I saw you and Grace with your mum this morning,' she says. 'Your *real* mum, that is.'

My heart misses a beat. I look round and see a triumphant smile appearing on her face, and realise she's uncovered another of my lies.

For a few seconds I'm lost for words but I know I've got to do something – something to stop her ruining everything.

I hurry into the hall where Abs, Freya and Ruby are sitting on the edge of the stage, waiting for me.

'What's the matter?' asks Ruby aghast. 'You look really upset!'

I glance back at Cait who's followed me into the hall.

I'm panicking inside now.

'It's . . . it's just . . . Cait. . .' I blurt out. I quickly stare at the floor so I can avoid their eyes. But I can't avoid hearing Dad's voice inside my head.

'You could act up for England,' he sneers.

'Has she been saying stuff again?' asks Abs.

'What's she said now?'

I take a deep breath then spit out the words.

'Something. . . about my Mum. . .'

'What?'

I bite my lip. 'I don't want to talk about it!'

And I really don't. What a performance. I think bitterly.

I turn my back on Cait. Abs, Freya and Ruby immediately do the same.

Well done, Drama Queenie. Result.

Cait looks like she's coming over, so now we deliberately cross to the other side of the hall, blanking her and making her look silly as she stands on her own. Freya and Ruby giggle. I dart a glance at Cait. She shoots it back, daggers drawn, and I know this is how it's going to be from now on.

War.

Chapter 42

Grace

Ryan is definitely avoiding me. But not just me. He's avoiding everyone. Kev and Darren want to know what's going on. We haven't rehearsed for days and Kev's pleading with me to talk to Ryan. With a nod I promise him I'll try, but at break Miss Turner keeps me behind to finish some work, so I don't get the chance. After break, in maths, neither Ryan nor PJ turn up. I look around the room puzzled. There's a weird atmosphere in here, like someone's shaken up a giant bottle of cola and it's fizzing everywhere.

'OK, where's Baxter and Jacobs?' Mr Harris asks, his bushy eyebrows scanning the class.

'Head's office,' calls Daisy Millar. 'They had a massive fight at break.'

I look up alarmed.

'Oh, marvellous,' sighs Hairy Harris.

'Yeah, it was brilliant, sir,' shouts Darren excitedly. 'And when Ryan smacked PJ in the mouth – blood everywhere!'

'Spare me the details, Darren,' replies Mr Harris, rolling his eyes. 'Right, settle down everyone, the excitement's over. Open your books, page two-three-four. Let's move on to the slightly less violent delights of algebraic equations.'

There's a groan from some of the class.

I look down at my textbook but the numbers and letters are swimming around on the page. I try to breathe slowly, to list something – anything – to calm me down, but it's no good. My stomach's churning as the image of Dad, angrily hitting Mum in the face with the full force of his fist, the night before we left home, explodes into my mind.

I clamp my hand to my mouth, leap up and dash towards the classroom door.

'Grace, are you all right?' Mr Harris asks.

I manage to shake my head before running to the girls' loos.

I batter my way into a cubicle, lean over the toilet and promptly throw up.

Chapter 43

Ellie

Everyone's talking about the fight – everyone except Cait who's keeping really quiet. No one's seen Ryan or PJ since break and there's a rumour going round that they've both been sent home and expelled, but then Grace and I see them coming out of the Head's office when the bell goes for the end of school.

When Grace sees Ryan she freezes, then turns around and quickly starts walking off in the opposite direction.

'Aren't you going to speak to him?' I ask, following her down the corridor.

She doesn't reply.

'Grace?'

'I can't talk to someone who hits people,' she says.

'But what about the band? Beachfest is in a few weeks.'

She shakes her head. 'I'm going home.'

She walks off and leaves me standing. I glance at Ryan, who watches Grace hurry away. He pulls a face then turns and heads off in the opposite direction.

In rehearsals, Cait keeps away from everyone, except for when she's on stage and playing her part. But there's something different about her too – something weird, like she's acting even when she's not on stage.

'What's going on?' I whisper.

'She's heartbroken,' says Freya sarcastically.

'PJ's been suspended for two weeks,' Abs tells me. 'And Ryan.'

'But what were they fighting about?' I ask.

'Daisy Millar saw PJ twisting Cait's arm behind her back. Ryan told him to pack it in, PJ went ballistic, lashed out and it all kicked off.'

'Then, can you believe it, Cait told Turner that PJ wasn't hurting her and he was just mucking about!' interrupts Ruby.

Poor Ryan, I think – I've got to tell Grace the full story as soon as I get home.

When the rehearsal's over, I rush back to the caravan, but Grace isn't there. Or Bruno. Realising she must have taken him for a walk, I head down to the beach but there's no sign of them there either. I run back to the caravan and I'm about to go inside when I suddenly get the strangest feeling that she's with the Maids. I hurry along the path and spot her, sitting like a statue in the middle of the stone circle, with Bruno nearby.

'Grace!' I call, 'it wasn't his fault!'

She looks up and stares back at me surprised, as I start to explain what happened at the fight.

'But why would Cait say they were just messing about if PJ was really hurting her?' she asks.

'Why do you think?' I say, astounded that someone who was supposed to be such a mega genius, could be so completely stupid. 'Why did Mum always pretend everything was OK?'

Grace pulls a face and stands up.

'I've got to talk to Ryan,' she says.

She hands me Bruno's lead and walks off.

Chapter 44

Grace

I hurry down into town to Ryan's house near the market square and knock on the door. I wait on the step for ages till finally I hear someone coming. Ryan's dad opens the door then slumps back in his wheelchair as if exhausted with the effort.

'He's not here, Grace,' he tells me, gasping in between each word. There are dark rings under his eyes.

I stand on the step, awkward and unsure what to do next.

'Mum!' I hear one of the twins call. It's Tom. He comes rushing down the hall but stops, disappointed when he sees me. His dad puts his arm around him as the small boy climbs onto his lap.

'It wasn't Ryan's fault, the fight, I mean . . .' I begin to explain.

'It's all right. I know my boy better than he knows himself. He does the right thing.'

'Where is he?'

'Up at Seal Point, I expect. He'll be back in a while. Come in and wait if you like.'

'Thanks,' I say, 'but I think I'll go and find him.'

'Tell him what I said,' his dad says, looking me straight in the eye. 'Tell him I know he does the right thing.'

I nod, then head off taking the cliff path, where I find Ryan sitting on the grass staring out to sea.

He smiles when he sees me but his eyes are sad. Trembling, I sit down next to him. The cliff edge doesn't seem so scary now.

'I'm sorry,' I murmur. 'Ellie told me about Cait and PJ.'

He shrugs. 'History.'

'You went to help her. I didn't know.'

'Couldn't exactly stand by and watch him pull her arm off.' He sighs. 'Better get home,' he says. 'Dad's not up to cooking.'

'It's only two weeks. You'll be back at school soon,' I tell him. 'Everything'll be back to normal.'

'No, everything's changed.'

'What do you mean?'

'I'm not going back.'

'What?'

'I'll be living in Scotland.'

'What are you talking about?'

'The twins and me. We're going to live with Mum.'

'But . . . but what about your dad?'

'He wants us to go. Won't take no for an answer. He's arranged for a carer to come in to help. Says it's for the best. Says he won't have us seeing him going downhill. He's going into hospital in a couple of days. They're going to pump him full of steroids.'

Ryan's quiet for a moment. I reach for his hand and hold it tight.

'He'll be OK,' I say.

'Maybe. He's been this bad before.'

'And he got better?'

'For a while.'

'When are you going?' I ask, my whole world falling apart

as if the cliff in front of us was dissolving into the sea below.

'Tomorrow.' There's a tremor in his voice. 'Grace, what do I do?'

My heart is breaking. I want to tell him to stay.

'Your dad said . . . he said . . . you do the right thing.'

'I don't want to leave him. I don't care how bad he gets. He's my dad.'

'Then stay.'

'But what about Harry and Tom? Mum walked out when they were less than a year old. ' He stops and shakes his head. 'They're going to need me too. They think living at Mum's is going to be one big holiday. They're already talking about hunting the Loch Ness Monster. She's got a two-bedroom flat in the middle of Glasgow.'

'Can't you talk to her?'

'Tried, last week. She's not the listening sort.' He looks at me. 'And then there's you, Grace. You're the best thing that's come into my life. I'm going to lose you too.'

Chapter 45

Ellie

Grace doesn't say anything when she comes back.

'Did you find him?' I ask.

She nods.

'That's good. So everything's OK then.'

She doesn't reply. She runs into our little bedroom, throws herself on the bunk and starts sobbing.

'Grace! What's wrong?'

I'm totally shocked. I've never heard her cry like this. Come to think of it, I've never even heard her cry before. Grace doesn't do tears. She certainly doesn't do noisy, unrestrained sobbing. Grace keeps calm and carries on. Always.

'What is it?' I plead. 'What's happened?'

'He's going away!' she whispers. 'Oh, Ellie!'

I hug her tightly and say all the reassuring things I can think of. Things she's said to me again and again in the past, when it's been the end of my world. It's ages before she manages to explain that Ryan's going to live with his mum in Scotland.

I rack my brains for something to make her feel better.

'You'll see him again,' I say brightly. 'Course you will . . .'

Suddenly I'm inspired. 'Hey, what about Gran and Grandad? They met by chance – a chance in a million – and then they had to go their separate ways. It only took them . . . five years to get back together. And Scotland's less than six hundred miles away and —'

Grace sobs louder and I get the feeling I'm not doing this right. I give it one last shot.

'Grace, it's going to be OK!' I say, wondering whether I should waft smelling salts under her nose like they do in those old black and white films on telly. But we're all out of salts, smelling, cooking, bath or anything else.

'Gracie, listen! I *know* it's going to be OK!' I insist.

Shocked at the fierceness in my voice, she looks up at me, her eyes red and her face so puffy it doesn't even look like hers any more.

'You've just got to trust!' I tell her firmly, sticking my chin out and doing the stiff upper lip thing. Her face crumples.

'But. . . I don't know how to . . .' she replies, then starts sobbing again.

I'm well out of my depth. I don't know what to do now.

When Mum gets home, she takes over. By bedtime Grace is quiet, the sort of quiet that comes when you're all cried out.

In the morning we walk to school but she doesn't talk to me other than to reply 'yes' or 'no' when I ask her something. I feel sorry for her at break and lunchtime – she sits on her own but shakes her head when I ask her to come and sit with me and my mates. She hardly eats a thing. And that's how it goes day after day.

After two weeks PJ comes back to school, and Cait hangs around with him again. Grace avoids him like the plague. She avoids everyone like the plague. Even me. She's still really quiet all the time, but she doesn't cry herself to sleep at night any more. Mum's worried she's not eating properly and brings home treats from the café to try and tempt her. My school trousers are really tight now.

And I'm too scared to ask her if she's heard from Ryan.

Chapter 46

Grace

They say you can get used to anything in time. But how much time? It's been over two weeks now since Ryan left. I've never felt anything like this horrible, hollow ache inside me. I check Mum's mobile every day in case he's texted or left a message.

Nothing.

It will get easier, I tell myself. It must. I just have to stop thinking about him and concentrate on other things. So I try. I really do. I make lists. Of anything and everything. Top ten songs, artists, ambitions – bottom ten teachers, phobias, bad habits. I make lists of my lists. I sew. I unpick and re-sew. I play my violin till my fingers are raw. I keep my head down at school, and after school today, bored and lonely, I creep into the hall to watch Ellie's rehearsal for the first time.

And I'm amazed at how good my little sister actually is. Dad's label of Drama Queen was totally perfect but not in the way he ever meant. Up on stage she shines, standing out from the other actors, even Cait, who's good, but not half as talented as Ellie.

I'm still not sure what's going on between the two of them

174

but now I see them together, it's obvious they're at war off stage as well as on.

At our last school, a group of girls used to gang up on me because I was different, an easy target. I didn't ever talk back, let alone fight back. I figured they'd get bored with no reaction and fortunately, after a couple of miserable months, I was right. They worked in a pack and their leader was a pretty doll-faced girl called Jessica Stribly, who had blond curly hair neatly tied up in a ponytail, a dainty up-turned nose and blue eyes with long lashes. She had convinced most adults that butter wouldn't melt in her mouth and spent the best part of two terms clawing her way to the top of the pecking order in our class.

By the time Ellie and I left, she didn't even have to say or do anything horrible, just the roll of her eye or a quiet dismissive tut was enough for her followers to do her dirty work, elbowing other girls accidentally on purpose, or firing taunts sharp enough to cut to the bone.

Even the hangers-on, the nice girls, got sucked in and fell under Jessica's spell. She was the one who decided who was to be spoken to, who was to be shunned and who was to be stabbed in the back. Sometimes she chose her victims logically – getting her revenge on girls who'd annoyed her – but occasionally her targets were totally random. She went after her scalps with the same dedicated passion other girls went shopping for shoes. And now, looking at my little sister, I'm alarmed to see that same cold, calculating look in her eye.

Somehow, over the last few weeks, while I've been lost in my own world missing Ryan, Ellie has climbed right to the top of the pack. Just like Jessica, she's the centre of attention, exactly where she's always wanted to be. She has a whole gang of followers. One has dyed her hair the same colour and another knots her tie exactly how Ellie does hers. All of them hang on her every word while Cait looks on from a distance.

When Ellie sees me she waves and comes over.

'We're trying on costumes now,' she tells me, like she's in charge or something. 'Why don't you hang around?'

Right on cue Mrs Mulligan appears with a huge pile of clothes in her arms. There's a flurry of excitement as she dishes out long flowing dresses, frilly shirts, weird hats and something she calls 'gentlemen's breeches'. She banishes the boys to a classroom opposite the hall so the girls can start getting changed. Seeing another pair of hands, she enlists my help and I spend the next few minutes wrestling Ellie into a beautiful silver brocade gown.

Cait eyes her jealously. 'Mrs Mulligan, I am supposed to be the Lady of the Manor,' she complains. 'This dress is totally rank.'

'Just put it on for now, Caitlin. Perhaps we can alter it if the fit's not very good,' Mrs Mulligan tells her as she hurries out of the hall to check on the boys.

'Let's face it, some people's bum would look big in anything!' Ellie quips loudly, eyeing Cait.

One of her friends lets out a snort of laughter.

'Oh this is rank!' the girl wails, imitating Cait.

'Quick, give her the elephant bum dress!' another girl calls.

'Can't – the elephant's already wearing it . . .'

'Why don't you all just shut up?' Cait snaps, but her outburst just provokes more laughter. I glare at Ellie but she shrugs back at me.

'It's all right, Grace,' she announces in an even louder voice, 'I'm not the only drama queen around here.'

Cait looks angrily at Ellie who stares her out.

'What's the matter, Cait?' asks one of the girls.

'Got some more rumours about me you want to spread around?' Ellie says, a cold gleam appearing in her eyes. 'Hey, I know, why don't you tell everyone about your lovely dolly collection? Better still, you could bring a few dollies in tomorrow and we could all play with them!'

Several girls explode into giggles. Some try to bite them back but the more they try, the more infectious the laughter becomes and soon everyone's involved. Cait's face crumples into the same pained expression that Ellie used to have when Dad said something nasty to humiliate her in front of other people.

She darts a glance at Ellie then turns and runs towards the hall doors. As she pushes them open, she catches her toe in the gaping hem of her long dress and trips through the doorway, provoking further snorts of laughter. I stare at Ellie, disgusted, but she doesn't even notice. The expression on her face is half triumphant, half shocked at the damage she's done.

I head out of the hall and find Cait hidden amongst the coats hanging in the cloakroom corridor. She's crying. I want to say something but before I can form a single word, she scrapes the tears from her face and snaps, 'What you staring at?' She pushes roughly past me and runs into the girls' loos.

Chapter 47

Ellie

'So what d'you think?' I ask Grace as we walk home along the path to the stones, after the rehearsal. She's not said a single word since we left school.

'About what?' she asks bluntly.

'Me, as Princess Caraboo.'

'Oh that. Yeah, you were all right.'

I zip up my jacket to keep out the cold. 'You didn't have to wait for me, you could have gone straight home.'

'It's not that.'

'Is it Ryan still?' I ask, shivering.

'No.' She stares at me and I suddenly feel uncomfortable.

'Then what?' I ask, putting my head down to avoid her eyes drilling into mine, because deep down I do know exactly what's bugging her. I just don't want to admit it.

'The way you treated Cait was horrible,' she starts to lecture, just like her old self. 'Ellie, how could you?!'

'The best form of defence is attack,' I retort.

'Who told you that – Dad?'

'What d'you mean?'

'Well, you were just like him today.'

'I was not!'

'Yes you were. When you had a go at Cait in front of everyone it was exactly like listening to him. You said the same sort of things he would.'

Memories of Dad hauling me in front of everyone in my cake-smeared dress flash into my mind and I can feel my face reddening with shame. Even my 'drama queen' taunt to Cait was below the belt. I remember Dad calling me that until he made me cry.

'I had to do it,' I tell Grace lamely. 'To protect ourselves.'

'What from, Ellie?' she asks me fiercely. 'Dad's not here now. Things are different.'

'Oh, you're so perfect, aren't you?' I snap back, angry with her, Dad and myself all rolled into one. 'Little Miss Wonderful! You never say a bad thing about anyone. Probably because you never say a single word in the first place!'

But she's already walking off. She leaves me standing between two stones.

'I don't care what I said to Cait,' I shout after her, 'she's not going to ruin everything. And what's more I don't give a monkey's what you think!'

I sit down on the ground, furious with everyone and everything. Even the way the rough grass prickles the backs of my legs through my school uniform irritates me. I push my back into the cold rough stone behind me. It jolts slightly and I tell it that it's just a stupid lump of rock, stuck in the ground by people who didn't have Xboxes or Facebook, and had nothing better to do.

It's getting dark now but I don't want to go back to the caravan and face Grace and then Mum, who will be kind and gentle and ask me what the matter is, and even though I don't want to, I'll end up telling her. So I stay right where I am, leaning against the stone, wondering what would happen if I never move from this spot.

Ellie, I tell myself, that's your stupidest, most bonkers idea of all your most stupid, bonkers ideas. Even if no one ever notices me sitting here in a pathetic little strop, I'll eventually starve. My decomposing body will be buried under grass and leaves and maybe in a hundred years' time someone will find a small pile of clean white bones and people will start making up tales about who I was and how I got here. One moment I'll be a Bronze-age human sacrifice, the next a wandering tramp frozen to death. And some bright spark is bound to think I was one of the Maids, who croaked it escaping from her stone prison. But no one will ever know the truth. No one will realise I was just a silly little girl who made up stories and told tales to everyone, especially herself.

I didn't like who I was before we left Dad and our old home but now I'm realising who I really am, I hate what I see. The brand new Elle Smith who everyone thinks is great! Who am I kidding? Grace is right. I'm not brand new at all, I'm just plain old Ellie Smith, the girl who's turned into her bully of a Dad. There's nothing great about that.

I check my watch. Dad will be home from work by now. Maybe the reason I'm always thinking about him is because we're so alike – two of a kind. My heart starts to beat faster as I fight to push thoughts of him out of my head. I don't want to be like him. Why can't I be like Grace or Mum, or Mum's parents? Even Dad's parents would be OK, I suppose. I've never seen them and they're both dead now, but Dad was always going on about how they were so perfect and did everything right and 'brought him up properly to the highest standards'. Why can't I have been like them?

A clammy sea fog is closing in all around me and I can hardly make out the outlines of the stones. In the cold misty twilight they seem to blend and melt and mingle, like they're moving, I think with a shiver.

Hypnotised, I watch them for maybe a minute, maybe an

hour – I don't know how long. Then out of the corner of my eye, I see them coming towards me. Two tall dark shapes and a little one. I let out a scream.

A bright light shines into my eyes and Mum, Grace and Bruno are by my side. Grace is holding a torch. They help me up then Mum hugs me tightly, the warmest, safest hug I've ever felt. Bruno nuzzles my legs but they're so numb they feel like they might give way any moment. Mum rubs my frozen hands in hers.

'Ellie, what on earth are you doing out here?' she asks.

Chapter 48

Grace

'Into that hot shower, right now,' Mum orders. 'You'll catch your death if you don't warm up.'

Ellie doesn't argue. I glance at her as Mum ushers her into the tiny bathroom. She looks different. I try to work out what's changed and finally realise the spark has gone from her eyes.

Mum heats up some soup and when Ellie is dressed and wrapped up in the quilt for extra warmth, we sit down together at the little table and eat the quietest meal we've had since we left Dad. Mum watches Ellie who keeps her head down as she slowly sips her soup.

Finally Ellie looks up and asks, right out of the blue, 'Mum, are you like your dad?'

'How do you mean?' she asks. 'Do I look like him?'

'No. Are you like him? Do you think like he did? Act like him?'

Mum pulls a face and shakes her head. 'Auntie Anna is more like your grandad than me.'

'So you're not like him?'

'He was the sort of person who wouldn't be pushed around.

Before he came to this country he spent most of his time standing up to people who could easily have had him killed. You've got to be made of strong stuff to do that.'

'You stood up to Miss Turner,' I say.

'Not quite the same thing,' Mum replies. She bites her lip and looks as if she might cry. 'Anna got cross with me once and told me I avoid confrontation like small boys avoid soap. But I suppose we are who we decide to be.'

'What do you mean?'

'Well, we're bound to have traits in us from our parents – same hair colour, say, or the shape of our nose. But we're not them. And we've got a choice in what we do. I remember Gran complaining that Grandad was so strong-headed and stubborn, but he'd just tell her that he and his dad clashed all the time. "*Jeden jaka druhy,*" he'd say. "One like the other." But they weren't the same. Gran told me the reason the secret police knew about that concert was that Grandad's dad had told them.'

'That's terrible!'

'He was a government official – part of the system. He did what he thought he had to.'

'Grandad must have hated him!' says Ellie.

Mum takes the quilt in her hands and points to a threadbare piece of green silk.

'This was part of the tie your great-grandad often wore. Grandad took it with him when he left for that concert. I think he knew that he'd never see his dad again.'

That evening, in our little bedroom, Ellie and I don't say a word to each other and the following day there's a really strange atmosphere between us as we walk to school in total silence. It's really weird for Ellie to be so quiet. We're like strangers instead of sisters. I don't see her during school and don't hang around for her while she's at rehearsal.

I walk out of school thinking about Ryan as usual, but

183

instead of going straight home I find myself heading down to the market, to his house, even though I know he's not there.

The place looks sad and forlorn. A couple of bodyboards have blown under a large straggly bush and grass is growing through the broken go-cart. I'm about to walk on when I see Ryan's dad coming along the pavement towards me.

'Grace,' he calls, 'how are you?'

I force a smile and nod. 'OK, thanks,' I mumble. 'How about you?'

'Stuffed full of pills, but apart from the rattle, can't complain.'

'And the twins? And . . . Ryan?' I hear myself ask.

Now it's his turn to paste on a smile. 'They were OK last week. They're starting new schools tomorrow. So I guess they've settled in.'

'That's good,' I say, biting back the tears.

'Yeah.' His voice is hoarse.

'Better go then.'

He nods. 'They'll be back in a month or so – just for a few days. Come round.'

'OK, thanks,' I say, knowing full well I won't.

He manoeuvres his wheelchair up the garden path, opens the front door and goes inside. I walk off down the road but as I turn the corner, a taxi passes. One of the passengers is waving madly at me but it takes a few seconds for me to realise that it's Harry. Shocked, I turn around and see the car pull up outside Ryan's house. The passenger doors fly open and Harry, Ryan and Tom pile out. The driver takes two suitcases from the boot as Ryan waves to me. It's only by clamping my hands over my mouth that I can stop myself crying out with joy.

'We're home!' Harry shouts. The two boys run up to their front door and knock noisily. Ecstatic, I rush back to meet Ryan, who runs along the pavement towards me and hugs me tightly.

'I've missed you, Grace,' he whispers.

'I've missed you too,' I reply, my voice choking.

Ryan's dad appears at their front door. 'What's going on?' he asks, confused.

Ryan doesn't take his eyes from my face as he says simply. 'It's OK, Dad. Mum's just changed her mind.'

His dad tries to look concerned but it's obvious he's delighted too.

'Well,' he says gruffly, after a few seconds. 'Well. That's her loss then.'

Ryan puts his arm around me and we all go inside. Out of the twins' earshot he explains that living with their mum was a disaster from day one. The intrusion of three wild boys had turned her ordered life, and her tidy two bed-roomed flat, upside down.

'But she definitely knows you're here?' His dad asks.

'She paid for the train fare and taxi,' says Ryan.

'I'm so glad you're home, son,' Ryan's dad tells him, his voice trembling with emotion.

'It's going to be OK Dad,' Ryan tells him. 'We'll manage.'

'Damn right, we will. Grace, get that pan on. I've got a flipping fridge full of sausages! '

So I start to cook tea while Ryan hurries round, unpacking, piling dirty washing into the washing machine, tidying and clearing up the kitchen. The twins sit on their dad's lap and he puts his arms around them like he's never going to let them go.

'It's a good job you're back,' he tells Ryan. 'I had to tell Mickey down the lifeboat station you weren't going to play at Beachfest, but there's nothing to stop you now. I'm counting the days, son. Counting the days.'

Chapter 49

Ellie

When Grace comes in I can hardly believe the change in her. It's like she's a completely different person, she's so happy. She makes up for saying practically nothing to me for the last three weeks by talking non-stop. After twenty minutes I tell her I'm really glad Ryan's back but I'm just going into our bedroom to do my homework. Mum looks at me, shocked, so out of Grace's sight I pull a gaga expression. Mum nods and smiles, understanding that for once Grace is doing my head in.

I don't sleep a wink all night thinking about what I'm going to do tomorrow and I don't think Grace does either. In the morning we're both up really early for school.

When we get there, she rushes off to find Ryan so I head across the playground, looking for Cait. I see her leaning against the wall near the science labs with PJ and one of his friends. She's wearing more make-up than usual and has fake tan over her face. The two boys are chewing over last night's football. Cait hovers by PJ's side, pretending to be interested. The bell rings for registration and she picks up her bag.

'Hang on,' he says.

She hesitates. 'I'll be late, PJ.'

'So?' he asks. 'Thought you liked being with me?'

'I do, but —'

'I'm the highlight of your day, aren't I?'

Cait looks uncomfortable as PJ and his friend exchange smirks.

'Yeah, well, don't bother meeting me later,' PJ adds.

'Why?' Cait asks surprised.

'Obvious, innit? Look at the state of you. More slap than Coco the Clown.' And with this he walks off with his mate, leaving Cait standing on her own.

She sees me but quickly looks away and hurries inside and down the corridor toward our form room.

Seeing my chance I run after her and catch her up. 'Cait . . .'

She turns and stares at me, angry and embarrassed. 'What?'

'I . . . I just wanted to talk to you.' I'm feeling nervous now.

'Really. Well, I don't want to talk to you.' She starts to walk off.

'Hang on.'

She stops and stares at me. 'Well?'

My mouth is dry and for once in my life I'm not sure what to say.

'I'm sorry,' I blurt out.

'For what, exactly?' she snaps.

'For . . . for everything, I suppose.'

She stares at me, unsure whether this is just another wind up.

'I mean it. I've been horrible.'

'Understatement of the year, Elle.'

'Look, I really am sorry. I mean it. I want to be mates again.'

'You're joking, aren't you?'

'No, I'm not. I've been thinking about stuff and —'

'Get lost, Elle.'

'Ellie,' I say, looking her in the eye. 'My name's . . . just plain Ellie.'

She stares back at me unnerved, unsure what to say or do. Our form teacher comes along and chivvies us both into class.

'Hurry up, girls. Bell's already gone,' he says as he follows us into the noisy classroom then bellows at everyone to be quiet.

Throughout registration Cait eyes me suspiciously. And this is how it goes for the rest of the day. A strange uneasy truce springs up between us. We're both unsure what's going to happen next so we give each other a wide berth while all the time secretly watching for one another's next move.

It's only in rehearsals that we actually communicate face to face. We have to. But now we've learnt our lines, we both already know exactly what we're going to say to one another and we also know each other's motives.

It doesn't take more than an hour or two for Abs, Ruby, Shareen and Freya to want to know what's going on, so I tell them the truth, or at least a short, edited version of the truth. I tell them I'm sorry how I've treated Cait and want to be friends again.

'You're wasting your time,' Abs tells me. 'Anyway she hangs around with PJ all the time. He's got her on a bit of string.'

Abs is right of course. Cait doesn't want anything to do with me but I'm still determined to be friendly.

I catch up with Grace, after school. While I've been rehearsing, she's been watching Ryan play in a football match.

'I don't want to be like Dad,' I tell her. 'And I'm not going to be.'

'So what about Cait?'

'I don't know how to make it up to her. I tried talking to her but she wouldn't listen.'

'Deeds not words then, I suppose,' Grace says with a shrug.

'What?'

'Maybe you should do something,'

'Like what?' I ask.

'Don't know. You'll have to work that one out.'

Suddenly I have an idea. An idea so brilliant that even Cait couldn't help forgiving me.

'You go on home, I'll see you later,' I tell her.

'What are you up to?' she asks.

'Just a quick deed,' I reply, running back inside the school building.

I cautiously open the door to the hall. Inside it's deserted and there's no sign of Mrs Mulligan.

I creep over to the costume rail and start flicking through them all until I find Cait's unflattering grey woollen dress. I check the coast is clear then quickly roll it into a ball and stuff it into my bag. I must be bonkers, I think – Mad Mulligan would chop me into a thousand pieces if she saw what I'm doing.

I hurry out of school but instead of going home I head down to town. It's quarter to five. I've got just fifteen minutes. I run along the high street until I get to the charity shop on the corner, then whizz inside and start rooting like a maniac through all the second-hand clothes hanging on the rails. The little old lady in charge tries to steer me towards stuff that would look OK on a teenager my size but I'm more interested in a patterned silk blouse size twenty-four and a faded blue velvet maternity dress.

She takes pity on me and lets me have both items for two pounds. I thank her and she throws in a vest top.

'This would look lovely on you dear,' she whispers. 'Much better than those other frumpy things. You really should watch one of those nice style programmes on telly. Pick up a few tips.'

Stifling a laugh, I thank her and head back to the caravan. Inside, Mum is busy cooking tea with Grace.

'Hi, Ellie, good day at school?'

'Great.' I dive into the little bedroom and shut the door behind me.

'What are you up to?' Mum asks.

'Nothing!' I reply. 'Just don't come in.'

Chapter 50

Grace

Ellie comes out for tea, gobbles it down, then straight after dives back into the bedroom.

'What are you doing in there?' Mum asks, trying to crane her head around the door.

'Homework . . . sort of,' Ellie replies, quickly closing the door on her.

Mum looks at me for more information.

'I don't know,' I tell her, 'but I don't think it's going that well.'

I'm right. Whatever she's up to is going pear-shaped. From time to time we hear ripping noises then growls and a few choice swear words.

In the end Mum's had enough.

'Ellie, come out here, right now.'

The door slowly opens.

'What *is* going on?'

Ellie pulls a face and shuts her eyes.

'A bloody great big disaster!' she wails.

'Ellie!'

I edge past them into the bedroom. It looks like an explosion in a rag factory. There are bits of fabric everywhere.

'It should be easy!' Ellie complains. 'You're always snipping up stuff, making lovely dresses and things.'

'Where did you get all that material?' Mum asks.

The remains of a grey woollen dress lying on the bottom bunk looks strangely like Cait's costume. My mouth drops open.

'Oh Ellie . . . you didn't —'

'Look, I did exactly what you do. I can't help it if it won't behave!'

'What's the matter?' Mum asks.

'It's OK,' I tell her. 'Maybe I'll just help Ellie for a bit.'

Mum goes out shaking her head as I pick up the grey dress. There are rips and tears and one of the arms is completely missing. The whole thing looks as if it's been in a fight with a shredder.

'I'm going to be in so much trouble,' Ellie says. 'Cait will think I've done it on purpose but I just wanted her to look good.'

'You should have asked me to help,' I tell her.

'But then it wouldn't have been *me* putting things right,' she protests. 'It would have been you.'

'Ellie, you stick to the brilliant ideas and let me handle the practical stuff,' I retort. 'It's called teamwork.'

I get Gran's sewing box down from the shelf and find a reel of grey thread and some pins. I make Ellie put on the dress so I can see better what needs to be done then hunt through the remains of the material for useable pieces. I cut off the other sleeve from the grey dress, tidy up the ripped one and then use the silk blouse to make new sleeves. With the rest of the silk I sew a panel for the front of the dress up to the neckline. Lastly, I cut up the velvet maternity dress to make an overskirt, gathering it slightly round the waist and tucking it under. Ellie is about Cait's size so I make a few nips and tucks to make the whole thing more flattering.

It takes ages because I'm doing everything by hand but finally it's finished. There's nothing else I can do and it's late.

'It's beautiful!' Mum gasps in surprise when we show her.

'Thank goodness for that,' I say, just slightly smugly, as Ellie takes off the dress and carefully folds it.

'Let's hope Cait likes it,' she says.

'Too late if she doesn't,' I retort.

We leave for school early the next day so we can return Cait's costume without anyone seeing us.

But as Ellie's placing it back on the rail, Mad Mulligan comes into the hall with a stack of wigs.

'What are you doing Elle?' she asks.

'Um . . . I . . . um, we . . . we've sorted Cait's dress.'

Anxiously Ellie holds up the dress as Mad Mulligan peers at it closely.

'You did this, Elle?'

'No, it was my idea, but Grace did all the sewing.'

'This is good, very good.'

'She wants to be a fashion designer, don't you?'

I nod, wishing I could say something. I might be able to talk to Mum, Ryan and his dad, as well as to Ellie now, but with anyone else I'm still struck dumb.

'In that case, maybe you'll help me out with some of the other costumes?' she asks.

I smile and nod and this seems to be good enough for Mad Mulligan.

She hands me another dress from the rail. 'This is supposed to be a ball gown, but it looks more panto than glam at the moment.'

I look at the dress and immediately know exactly what I'd do to improve it.

'Well, what d'you think?' she asks.

I want to tell her my plan but as usual no words come out. I can feel my face reddening with embarrassment and frustration.

'Erm . . . Grace doesn't talk much,' Ellie mumbles after a few moments.

'Oh . . . OK,' Mulligan says as if this were the most normal thing in the world. 'Well . . . fair enough, it's your design skills I'm interested in. A lot of these costumes are going to need tarting up and I just don't have the time, but if you help, Grace, we'll photograph everything and put together a professional portfolio for you. It'll help get you into a good art college when you leave here.'

As the bell rings for the start of school, she tells me I can work in her office any time I want and also have a small budget for buying all materials I need. Best of all, she promises to get hold of a sewing machine which she'll show me how to use.

'I'm really sorry for dropping you in it, Grace,' Ellie whispers as we head out of the hall. 'I didn't mean that to happen.'

But I'm in my element. I can't wait to get started.

Chapter 51

Ellie

'Miss, it's gorgeous!' Cait says, twirling around in her new improved dress. 'I can't believe it!'

'Well, you've got Elle and her sister to thank. It was her idea and Grace did all the sewing,' Mad Mulligan tells her.

Cait's jaw drops open as she stares at me in astonishment.

'Grace will be helping out with some of the other costumes so —'

'Miss! Miss! Can she sort mine, Miss – ple-ase!' Ruby begs.

'And mine!' calls another girl.

Suddenly Mad Mulligan is surrounded by half the cast, all pleading to have their costumes upgraded. As she tries to restore some sort of order, Cait comes over to me, the skirt of her dress swishing as she walks.

'You look good,' I tell her nervously.

'Thanks.'

There's an awkward pause. I toe a white line on the hall floor as she hovers nearby.

'Want to go into town later?' I blurt out before I have time to change my mind.

'I'm meeting PJ,' she replies.

'Another day then?'

She shrugs. 'Yeah . . .'

I turn away disappointed. It's obvious she's just fobbing me off.

'Whatever. . .' I mumble, as if I don't care at all.

'I would but . . . but PJ doesn't like me hanging around with other people.'

She gives me a tight smile then her eyes dart to the back of the hall. One of the doors is open slightly and I can see him, coming down the corridor.

'Better go,' she says.

I watch as she hurries over to him. She twirls around in her dress but his reaction is lukewarm and although she tries to hide it, the disappointment shows on her face. He picks up one of the wigs from the box and plonks it on her head the wrong way round, getting a laugh from a couple of the boys nearby. She pulls it off but doesn't say anything. He tells her to stop sulking, he's only joking . . . even though she looks better with it on.

A few minutes later Mulligan calls us all to get in our places, ready to begin rehearsing. Dressed up in our costumes, the excitement spreads through the cast like electricity as Mulligan encourages, persuades and bullies us all into better and better performances. But I don't care if she shouts – I'm enjoying every minute. And even though Cait and I still aren't friends like we used to be, a rush of happiness floods through me, and for the first time ever, I realise I don't want to be anyone else any more. Plain old Ellie Smith suits me fine.

And I'm not the only one who's changed. Grace gets busy with the costumes both at home and school and the ones she finishes are totally amazing – they're bold and imaginative – like something off a catwalk. Most days now, the caravan is festooned with long dresses, cloaks and hats. Mum's pretty good about the place being turned into a costume factory and even helps Grace with the sewing sometimes, singing along to tunes on the radio as she works. As promised, Mad Mulligan has helped Grace photograph each one and she's mounted them all professionally and put them in a special portfolio. I told Grace she should make a list of them all but she just looked at me as if I were bonkers and said, 'Life's too short for lists, Ellie!' And then she laughed.

After school, and at weekends, when she's not sewing costumes, she's at Ryan's rehearsing for Beachfest. There are posters all around town now and the local radio station is advertising it every day. Abs, Ruby and I have already got our tickets and everyone at school's talking about it. Grace let me watch one of their rehearsals last Saturday at the community hall, and I couldn't believe how good The Damage were.

On the way back we bumped into Susan. She asked how my stories were going. I didn't want to tell her, but basically they're not. I stopped writing a couple of weeks ago.

'When I re-read them, they just sounded stupid,' I finally admitted.

'Don't give up,' she replied. 'Write what's real to you. Something you know about.'

'I'm only thirteen. What do I know about anything?' I replied jokily.

It was only after we got back to the caravan, I realised I did have a story to tell, but one that I'll never in a million years let anyone else read.

I started a few days ago, secretly writing about Dad, putting down everything I can't tell anyone about in that purple patterned notebook. When I finish a few pages, I close up the book and hide it under my bunk, and it feels good because it's as if I've put him away too, so I can forget him for a while and get on with my life.

Chapter 52

Grace

It's the day before Beachfest and I'm getting nervous even though we've rehearsed our socks off for the last few weeks. We've got one final practice this evening, and then that's it.

'You'll be fine,' Ellie tells me as we walk home after school. I'm carrying the last costume Mad Mulligan wants altered – Ellie's – and planning to work on it before I go to Ryan's, or as Ellie calls it, my second home.

'Just make sure you do something extra special with it,' Ellie tells me. 'I want to look really glam!'

'OK, how about a great big bottom bustle in custard yellow and some giant lime green shoulder pads out to here?' I joke, holding my hands a metre apart.

'Don't even think about it,' she warns me.

The door to the caravan is open. Bruno is tied up outside and looks at us dolefully as we give him a quick cuddle.

'Mum must have left work early,' Ellie says. 'Hope she's bought something nice back for tea —'

We step inside the caravan and freeze in horror. Dad is sitting at the little caravan table. Mum is in the seat opposite him. All that divides them is a teapot, two mugs and a plate of Hobnobs. She's sitting perfectly still with a fragile smile on her lips but as Dad turns to us, I see a wild, fearful look escape from her eyes.

'What the hell have you done to your hair?' Dad snaps at Ellie, as if he last saw her this morning. 'That muck better wash out, young lady. You look like a freak!' He turns back to Mum and demands, 'What sort of mother lets her daughter go around looking like that?'

None of us says a word. Ellie bites her lip. There is a deathly silence.

'Great. You haven't seen your dad for weeks and you both stand there like a couple of stuffed dummies.'

'What are you doing here?' asks Ellie finally, with a tremor in her voice.

'What does it look like?' he retorts. 'Your mum and I are having a nice cup of tea.'

I glance at Mum but she avoids my eye, quickly looking down at her untouched mug.

'Well, this is all very nice, isn't it?' he adds.

No one replies.

'Isn't it, Karin?'

Mum nods.

'I've had one hell of a drive today, what with the car playing up and overheating, so I've decided we'll go home tomorrow evening when you two get back from school and I've had a bit of a rest.'

'Home? But -'

'The holiday's over,' he insists. 'I've forgiven your mum and everything's sorted.'

Still Mum doesn't speak. Inside I'm crying out for her to shout and stamp and stand up to him.

'*Mum?*' Ellie pleads quietly as we both look to her to do something.

'Tell them, Karin,' Dad orders. 'And you can give me your car keys too. I'll keep them nice and safe till tomorrow.'

Mum opens her bag and hands over her car keys. As she struggles to speak, I know from the look on her face what she's going to say before the words come out. My heart sinks as all our hopes and plans and dreams crumble to dust around us.

'We're going . . . back,' she whispers.

'Course we are!' Dad snaps. 'It's high time things returned to normal.'

'But we can't!' Ellie protests. 'Grace is playing in a festival and I'm in the school play next week.'

Dad gives a little hollow laugh. 'I'm sure they'll do just fine without our little Drama Queen prancing about on stage looking ridiculous, and Grace is talented enough to play in any number of concerts back home.'

'But —'

'No buts, Ellie, I don't want to hear another word.'

'I'm not going,' she says timidly.

He glares at her. She shrinks back.

'What?' His voice is quiet now.

She falters a little, knowing what she's doing is dangerous. 'What did you say?'

She takes a deep breath. I can't help silently urging her on. 'I'm not going.'

Dad's lips purse together and his eyes narrow. 'You'll do as I say.'

Mum starts to fidget. 'Course she will, Adam. It's OK, Ellie doesn't mean it, do you? Your dad's right, there'll be lots of other plays and concerts back home. Tell him you don't mean it, Ellie. There's a good girl.'

'I do mean it!' Ellie protests. 'I'm not going back!'

'Ell-ie . . . please, ' Mum pleads, eyeing Dad fearfully, as his grip tightens on his mug of tea.

Instinctively, she stands up. But she's too late – Dad lobs the mug at Ellie. It hits her arm hard and scalding tea splashes over her before it smashes on the floor.

Ellie bites back a yelp of pain and runs into our bedroom.

'Leave her!' Dad orders Mum, grabbing her wrist and twisting it as she attempts to follow her. He turns to me. 'And what about Grace? What have you got to say?'

Petrified, I stare at him dumbly, my thoughts churning as my face remains a mask. My mouth is dry and I feel sick. I've got a hundred things I want to say but I'm too frightened to make one little sound.

'That's settled then. Now how about something to eat? I'm tired and I'm hungry. Ellie can stay in that room all evening. I don't want to see her sulky little face.'

He sits back down again, taking out a postcard from his shirt pocket as Mum hurries to prepare his tea. I glance over and recognise the circle of stones. When he turns the postcard over, I see it's addressed to Auntie Anna in Ellie's handwriting.

'Took this out of your dozy cow of a sister's letter box, before she even saw it,' he tells Mum. 'You should tell her to get the lock mended on that box. Anyone could nick stuff from there.' He gives a dismissive tut and adds, 'Dancing Maids! What utter baloney!'

Chapter 53

Ellie

I lie here in my little bunk under the covers, secretly writing in my purple notebook. It's getting late now, half nine.

'I sneaked this when he wasn't looking,' Grace says handing me half a cold pasty. In the other room we can hear Dad's voice. I nibble at the crust but I'm not hungry any more. Grace looks out of the tiny caravan window into the darkness.

'You missed your rehearsal,' I tell her.

'I know. Thank goodness Ryan didn't turn up here looking for me. Dad's already angry enough.'

'But how did he find us?'

She pulls a face and avoids my eye and then I remember the postcard.

'It's my fault, isn't it? I sent a card to Auntie Anna.'

'He's brought it with him.'

I bury my face in my hands as I hear his triumphant voice in my head. *I'll always find you out, Ellie. Always.*

'I'm sorry, Grace.'

'He would have found us anyway.'

'Do you think?'

'Course,' she mumbles. 'How's your arm?'

I roll up my sleeve and see a massive bruise coming up. The skin around it is red and feels sore where the tea scalded me.

'He can't make me go,' I tell her. 'I'll run away or something but I'm not going back with him.'

'But what about Mum?' Grace asks, looking at me fearfully. I give a long deep sigh. We both know running away is not an option.

Throughout the night I have horrible dreams about Dad, and keep hearing his voice, low and threatening. At one point I wake with a jolt, sure that I've heard a stifled yell. I listen hard, but the sound of my own heart pounding is all I can hear before I drift back to sleep again.

In the morning Mum wakes us both. Her eyes are dull but her voice is artificially cheerful.

'Come on, you'll be late for school.'

'Mum —'

'Please, Ellie,' she whispers, wincing in pain and slowly moving her elbow closer to her ribs.

'What's wrong?' asks Grace.

'Nothing. I'm fine,' she replies with a forced smile and we both know he's hurt her.

'Don't say anything about your dad today, will you?' she begs in a chilling whisper, exactly like she used to.

'But —'

'It'll make things worse, Ellie. Promise me.'

'Where's the quilt?' Grace mouths suddenly with a look of panic on her face.

'It's OK, I've hidden it,' Mum whispers back.

'We can't just disappear,' I say. 'What about the café?'

'It's my day off today. But I'll ring Stan, tell him . . . something.'

'We don't want to leave you here on your own,' Ellie whispers.

'I'll be fine. Don't worry.'

Dad appears in the doorway behind her.

'Course she'll be all right,' he says. 'As long as you don't go telling any silly tales,' he threatens, glaring at me.

We set off for school in silence. As we walk through the circle of stones, I give a little shiver. It seems weird that after today we might never see them again. Our old life, a horrible distant memory, is going to become real again soon, and everything here will be just a wonderful but faraway dream. The hopelessness of it all sinks in. Grace, Mum and I have stopped dancing and are being turned back to stone.

My costume sits folded in the bottom of my school bag. Grace obviously didn't work on it last night, but it doesn't matter now because I won't be wearing it next week. I also tucked my purple patterned notebook into my bag with the rest of my school stuff, scared that Dad might go poking around my things, find it and read it. I couldn't risk that – he'd go ballistic.

'What are you going to tell Ryan?' I ask Grace as we reach the school gates. She shrugs her shoulders and doesn't reply. We go our separate ways.

In class, everyone's excited about Beachfest tonight and Abs and Ruby make complicated plans about what they're going to wear and where they'll meet me. I nod, not having the heart to tell them I won't be there. I can't bear to think how Grace is feeling right now.

At the dress rehearsal during the lunch hour, I forget my lines three times and Mad Mulligan throws a wobbly. She's also disappointed that Grace hasn't managed to do anything with my costume.

'Something came up last night,' I say.

'Well, there's still plenty of time before next week's performance, thankfully. Time enough for you to get your act together and for Grace to sort your costume.'

But she's wrong. Our time has almost run out.

Chapter 54

Grace

'What happened?' asks Ryan. 'Where were you last night?'

'I . . . couldn't make it . . . I'm sorry.' I force a smile but can feel my face cracking so I turn away and open my locker and pretend to sort out my books.

'You OK?'

I nod.

A book drops to the floor. My hand's shaking. I tuck it behind my back as Ryan picks up the book and pops it back in my locker for me.

'You don't seem OK,' he says.

'I'm fine. Really.' I fight to keep my voice steady.

'You've got that same look you had when I first met you. Like you're watching out for something.'

'I couldn't get away. That's all.' I'm desperate to change the subject. 'Kev sorted his intro on the first song?'

'Grace. You can talk to me. You can tell me anything.'

'Maybe he needs to pitch it lower.'

'What are you so scared of?'

'Nothing. Please, Ryan . . . Just leave me alone!'

We're both surprised by the emotion in my voice. Neither of us was expecting it.

'Sorry. I didn't mean . . .'

The hurt in his voice cuts me deep. I don't know what to tell him, so I'm silent. We stand together, but, for the first time in weeks, miles apart.

'Here,' he says at last, holding out a little package wrapped in foil. 'The lumps are toffee, not gravel.'

I stare at the misshapen package.

'Twins made them with Dad last night,' he says. 'They called them biscuits. The jury's still out.'

I bite back the tears prickling in my eyes as I realise in a few short hours I'll never see Ryan or his lovely family again. And when Beachfest is in full swing tonight, we'll be on our way home and I'll have let Ryan down completely.

'Tell them . . . thank you and . . .' I can feel Ryan's eyes on me. I want to say goodbye but I can't. 'Just thank them for me.'

'You will be OK for tonight, won't you?' he asks hesitantly.

I can't lie to him. But I can't tell him the truth. I mumble an excuse about having to meet Ellie and hurry away. I'm dying inside when I glimpse Ryan's bewildered expression as he watches me go.

'See you later then,' he calls.

I spend the rest of the day avoiding him but unable to think about anyone else. At lunchtime I hide out in Mad Mulligan's office with Ellie's costume on my lap pretending to sew it, freezing at every sound from the corridor. Even though there's no point, I force my needle in and out, barely registering what I'm doing as I prick my fingers, getting smears of red blood onto the silver fabric.

As soon as school finishes I find Ellie in the cloakroom, ready to go home.

'Have you told Ryan we're leaving?' she asks.

I hang my head.

We're walking towards the front doors when Mad Mulligan spots us and calls, 'Elle, where are you going?'

'Um . . . home, Miss. Think I'm coming down with something.'

'You'll live. Come on, get a move on, we're rehearsing in five minutes. No, four minutes and counting . . .'

Ellie darts me a look. 'I'll have to go,' she says. 'Make sure Mum's OK. I'll be back as soon as I can.'

Chapter 55

Ellie

Everyone's already costumed up and chatting excitedly or rehearsing moves and lines together. Only Cait stands apart with PJ, just inside the hall. As I walk in, he pushes her away from him, calling her a dumb cow. She bumps into me then spins out of the hall and rushes down the corridor.

Seeing Cait disappear, Mad Mulligan throws her hands into the air in theatrical despair.

'Elle, will you please go and get Caitlin Trelawny back here, right now!' she calls. 'In case she hasn't noticed, we have a play to perform in less than a week!'

I turn and hurry out of the hall, following Cait into the girls' loos.

'Cait?' I call. 'You OK?'

'Course I am,' she snaps, wiping her face with the palms of her hands. 'Why don't you just mind your own business for once?'

She goes to the sink, splashes cold water on her eyes and then glares at me. 'And don't you dare tell anyone I've been crying,' she adds, as if her eyes weren't a big red giveaway.

She turns to go.

'Cait.'

'What?'

'I . . . I need to tell you something.' I blurt out.

'Like what?'

My heart's thumping, but before I leave, I need to do this one last thing. I have to talk to her. If I don't speak now I'll always remember this moment and hate myself forever.

'It's a secret.'

'Then why are you telling me?'

'Because. . . because I'm not going to be here tomorrow.'

'Yeah right, off to Hollywood, are you?'

'Back to London.'

She looks at me surprised. 'What about the play?'

I shrug. 'You'll get to be Princess Caraboo and it'll be great.'

'Don't tease me.'

'I'm not. I'm deadly serious.'

'So why are you leaving now?'

'My dad's found us.'

'Found you? What you going on about?'

'I didn't tell you the truth before. I'm sorry – really sorry. I've told so many tales, stupid stories – and been so mean to you, I'm not surprised you hate me. Dad's not an actor – he works in an office. We ran away, Mum, Grace and me.'

'Ran away?'

'Everyone thinks he's great, but he's not. We left because he beat up Mum again.'

'You're just making this up, aren't you?' Cait tells me with disbelief. 'This is another one of your stories.'

'No. I swear. Until now, I've never told anyone the truth about Dad. I'm so scared and ashamed of him. I don't want anyone to know what he's really like.'

'I don't believe you.'

I roll up my sleeve. The bruise on my arm is purple and angry.

The surrounding skin is blistered and red raw. Cait looks at it in shock and repulsion.

'Did he do that?'

I nod.

'Ellie, you've got to tell a teacher, someone who can do something about this.'

'I can't. I promised Mum. And if Dad finds out I've said anything, even to you, he'd . . . he'd . . .' My voice trails away. I don't want to think about what Dad might do.

'So why are you telling me?'

'Because . . . we were friends once.'

I look down at the ground, knowing that this isn't the only reason. I struggle to find the right words. 'What's going on with PJ and you,' I tell her, 'it's the same thing. Just starting.'

She stares at me shocked, as if I've slapped her. 'PJ?'

'That horrible way he talks to you, and makes fun of you all the time, but nasty, like he wants to upset you and the way he tries to control your life. I've seen it all before with my dad . . . and worse.'

She looks down but I can see her face reddening and I wonder if PJ's ever hit her.

'It's too late for us,' I tell her, 'but you can stop it happening to you.'

Finally she looks up at me. 'It's not too late. But you've got to tell. Talk to Mulligan. Straight after rehearsals.'

'I can't.'

'You must.'

We head back to the hall together. Inside everyone's waiting. PJ calls to Cait but she doesn't answer him. She doesn't turn around. From the corner of my eye I see him scowl at her and mutter under his breath. I glance at Cait and she gives me a tight little smile.

'You've been a right pain in the butt, Ellie Smith, but I don't actually hate you, by the way,' she whispers.

'OK everyone, can we start rehearsing now, please?' Mad Mulligan asks.

I try my hardest to forget about Dad and just concentrate on the play for one final time. Whatever happens, I might as well enjoy this last hour on stage, doing what I love best.

I put everything I've got into the performance and Cait is amazing too. She loses all the awkward girliness she had before and suddenly she's totally convincing. We run through the whole play and Mulligan is ecstatic as we finish the last scene.

'We are going to that drama festival!' she announces triumphantly. 'Bring it on!'

When she dismisses us all, Cait hurries over to me.

'Now,' she urges. 'Go on. Tell her.'

Mad Mulligan is busy collecting up bits of costume. With Cait watching, I head over to her.

'Miss, can I speak to you for a minute, please?' I ask nervously.

'Is it very important, Elle?' she asks, balancing several hats on top of the pile of boots she's carrying. 'I've got to label all these hats and a pile of props to sort through.'

'Well, yes, it is.'

'OK, what's up?'

I look around the hall. There are still several people milling about.

'It's kind of private.'

We head down to her office. She dumps the things she's carrying onto her desk.

'Fire away, Princess Caraboo,' she jokes.

And now it comes to the moment I'm not sure how to start. Mulligan gives me a big bright smile while trying unsuccessfully to hide her impatience.

'Well?' she asks, picking up a hat and examining its wide brim. 'Last minute nerves, is it? That's perfectly normal. When I was at drama school, everyone was up in the air for at least three weeks before a performance. More nerves the better, I say. But you mustn't let them get to you. Just turn them to energy and channel it into your acting.'

'It's my dad,' I say finally.

'He's the actor, isn't he? In America?'

'No. I . . . I made that up.' I can feel my cheeks burning red.

'Oh.' She looks at me curiously. 'Right.'

It all tumbles out now. All about Dad and how we ran away and how he's found us now. Mulligan takes a deep breath then looks me in the eye.

'Elle, are you sure everything you've told me is completely true? You're not just exaggerating a little? Embroidering things a bit?'

She starts rambling on about how she and her dad didn't get on when she was a teenager.

'We had some right humdinger rows, I can tell you. But it's amazing what a few years and calming those hormones does. We're best buddies now. Even let me choose his nursing home.' She gives a bonkers little laugh and I can tell she thinks I'm making a fuss over nothing. But even if she did believe me I suddenly realise, what would she do? She isn't called Mad Mulligan for nothing. The bruise on my arm feels sore but there's no point showing her.

'Forget it,' I say, 'I have to go. I'm sorry, Miss, you're right. I shouldn't have said anything.'

'Elle?' she calls after me.

'Ellie.' I tell her. 'My name's really just plain Ellie.'

I rush out of her office, into the playground and through the school gates. And it isn't until I'm almost back at the caravan that I realise I've left my school bag in the hall.

Chapter 56

Grace

I don't go straight home from school. My head is on fire as thoughts of Ryan, Dad, Mum and Ellie batter from corner to corner in my mind. I head for the beach, hoping the fresh sea air will allow me to breathe and stop the choking feeling in my throat. The wind is blowing hard but the sun feels hot as I climb the cliff path and sit on the same bench I sat with Ryan that day he rescued Bruno. The thought of letting him down tonight is tormenting me but knowing that I'll never see him again is unbearable.

Feeling desperate, I peer over the cliff edge and shiver, not wanting to acknowledge the horrible thoughts worming their way into my mind, whispering to me that if I just stepped out a few paces everything could be over in a few seconds . . . whereas going back home with Dad would be a life sentence.

From the corner of my eye I see two sleek dark heads bobbing between the waves - mermaid seals, with pearls for tears. They swim around the rocks without a care in the world. Lucky them, I think. I sit for ages watching them and only gradually realise it's getting late and I should be home.

I hurry back, panicking slightly as I anticipate Dad's anger. Inside the caravan, Mum is packing up the last of our things. Ellie's here but there's no sign of Dad.

'He's had to take the car to a garage in town,' she tells me, quickly taking Gran's quilt from a compartment under one of the bench seats, folding it and putting it carefully in the bottom of her holdall. 'He'll be back in half an hour.'

The caravan door swings open. Mum reaches for the bag as Dad walks in.

'What's in there?' he asks suspiciously, seeing the look of panic etched on her face.

'Just a few bits and pieces,' she replies brightly, standing to attention but avoiding his eye.

He snatches the holdall from her and tips out the contents. His expression darkens when he sees the quilt.

'And what the hell is this doing here?'

Mum glances at Ellie and me to warn us not to say anything. 'Well? I'm waiting.'

'I . . . I took it out of the bin.' Mum's trembling now.

'Oh you did, did you? And who gave you permission to do that? Why d'you think I threw it away in the first place?'

He bundles it into a ball when suddenly Mum's phone rings. She stares at it surprised but doesn't pick it up.

'Full of secrets aren't you? Got yourself a new boyfriend, too?'

He grabs the phone and answers it. 'Yes,' he snaps.

As he listens to the voice on the other end of the line, he looks slightly taken aback. His tone of voice changes to warm and pleasant.

'I'm afraid she's not here at the moment. Perhaps I can take a message? . . . Tomorrow? . . . And what's it about? . . . Fair enough. Tomorrow then. Goodbye.'

He ends the call and looks at Mum.

'A Miss Turner wants to see you in school tomorrow.' He

glares at Ellie and me. 'What's going on?'

'Grace was in trouble for missing her detention a few weeks ago,' Ellie says. 'Mum's already seen her once.'

'Grace in detention! I could understand Drama Queenie here, but Grace?' He jabs a finger at Mum. 'You see what you've done, bringing my children to this dump? They used to behave themselves back home!'

'I'm sorry, Adam,' Mum mumbles.

'She sounds like a right old bag. I hope she tears you off a strip.'

'But . . . aren't we going home tonight?' Ellie asks.

'And that's another thing,' he snaps, rounding on Mum again. 'The stupid garage is waiting for a gasket to arrive. I can't pick up the car until tomorrow evening. Thanks to you, I'm going to have to take yet another day off work.'

He flings the quilt across the room where it lands in a crumpled heap next to Bruno, who whimpers. Like us, very soon the quilt will be gone from here. Dad will get rid of it and this time he'll make absolutely sure we can't rescue it.

I look at it lying on the floor and feel sad until it slowly dawns on me that Dad's too late; we've already heard its stories. They're no longer secret; they're a part of us now. A wave of triumph floods though me. Although I stand frozen next to Mum and Ellie, I'm dancing inside because I know Dad can't take those tales away from us. Tomorrow we'll have to go back with him, but we're going to be here for the next twenty-four hours. More than enough time for me to make another story – all of my own.

Chapter 57

Ellie

Mum has made steak and onion pie for tea. I sit up straight at the caravan table careful not to let my knees knock into Dad's, getting cramp in my leg instead.

'It's your favourite,' Mum tells him hopefully, as if the huge piece of pie on his plate might somehow calm him down.

'Pastry's burnt,' he grumbles but he eats it all the same.

I try my best not to spill any peas or let a single flake of pastry escape onto the table so Dad has no reason to shout at me, but Grace just pushes her food around her plate with her fork. Mum shoots a warning glance at her.

'All right, love?' she asks quietly.

Grace looks down and doesn't reply.

'Worried about that Miss Turner, very likely,' says Dad. 'And so you should be, young lady. You can reap your reward, learn your lesson, so when we do get home we'll have the old Grace back. Now eat up.'

But she puts down her fork, rubs her hand across her stomach and pulls a face.

'I don't think she's feeling well, Adam. It's probably her . . .

you know. Do you want to lie down, Grace?'

She nods then goes into our little bedroom.

'Bloody women! There's always something the matter with you,' says Dad, forking in another chunk of pie.

As soon as I can, I follow Grace into our room. She's lying in her bunk under her duvet even though it still feels warm in our room.

'What's wrong?' I ask.

With her eyes, she motions to me to close the door. As I click it shut, she quietly drops down from the bunk. She's not wearing her school uniform — she's put on her favourite flowery hippy dress and her raspberry coloured jumper. Silently she takes her school uniform and bag and makes a Grace-shaped bolster on her bed before covering it with the duvet.

She picks up her violin and bow then opens the window. 'You don't know anything, OK? You think I'm asleep, right here under the covers,' she insists. 'I'll be back as soon as I can.'

'Dad'll kill you if he finds out.'

She looks at me, deadly serious. 'It'll be worth it.'

Carefully, she squeezes herself through the window and drops down onto the ground. She hitches up her skirt in one hand and with her long hair blowing in the wind, runs off toward the beach as I'm yelling inside my head, 'Go, Grace! Go!'

I slip quietly back into the other room. Dad's watching a film on television while Mum's washing the dishes. Her hand's shaking as she carefully lowers the plate she's just rinsed onto the draining board, but it slips and drops to the floor with a loud crash.

'For goodness' sake, woman!' Dad yells. 'Can't you even wash up properly?'

Mum doesn't answer but the next cup she washes, she puts down as if it were a hand grenade.

'How's Grace?' she asks me quietly a few minutes later.

'Think she's asleep.'

216

'I'm trying to listen to this!' Dad growls, without taking his eyes off the telly. Which is just as well because he doesn't see the secret smile on my face.

Suddenly, the caravan is full of music. Dad looks round to tell Mum off again but realises the sound is coming from outside.

'What the hell's that racket?' he asks, peering out of the window.

Chapter 58

Grace

The beach is packed. The stage is lit up with coloured lamps that throw their light onto the crowd below, bathing them in red, green and blue. The whole school and half the town is here. I weave my way around groups of people, looking for Ryan. Finally I spot him on the far side, standing with Kev and Darren who look totally downcast as Ryan scans the crowds, searching for some sign of me.

I wave and eventually he sees me. He nudges the others, who grin in relief, and then hurries over.

'I knew you'd come,' he whispers, taking my hand. 'You're cold.'

I'm shaking. But not with cold.

'We're on next,' he says, putting his jacket around me. 'Come on.'

He leads me to where Kev and Darren are waiting and then we all make our way to the back of the stage, just as the first band are finishing their last song.

As they bound off, the MC gives a speech about how important the lifeboat station is and how the money raised

218

from Beachfest will help to keep it running, while we quickly take their place and get ready to play.

'And now . . . Put your hands together for our first local band tonight – The Damage!'

We start our first song and within seconds the crowd love us. To one side, at the front, I spot Ryan's dad with the twins on his lap.

Both the twins wave at me furiously and don't stop even when I mouth hello and smile back. Ryan's dad has tears in his eyes but a huge grin on his face. I glance over at Ryan, who smiles proudly back at me.

We've just begun our second and final number, when suddenly my heart misses a beat as I spot a figure in the distance marching down from the caravan site. Even in the dull moonlight I realise it's Dad. Any moment now he'll see me.

My first thought is to run off stage before he spots me and somehow try to get back to the caravan undetected. I glance at Ryan who grins back at me unaware anything's wrong. I take a deep breath and stay exactly where I am. As I play on, I watch Dad thread his way through the crowd, coming nearer and nearer, until I can see his face, his expression set hard like concrete. And now he's here, standing in front of the stage, staring straight at me with a fixed smile on his face but his eyes like thunder, as the crowd calls for an encore.

'Fantastic! Let's hear The Damage one more time!' echoes the MC.

Dad nods to me to get off the stage.

I stare back at him then tuck my violin – my grandad's violin – under my chin and take his bow and launch into the song again. This time I'm playing for Grandad and for Mum, for Ellie and for me. I play louder and bolder than before. I play defiantly. The music takes over, nothing else matters. I look out at the crowd and suddenly realise that everyone is dancing – everyone except Dad. Safe in the song, I desperately want it to last forever, but all too soon it finishes.

As we step down from the stage, Dad is waiting for me a few metres away.

'I have to go,' I tell Ryan.

'What's wrong?'

'My dad's here.'

'I'll come and say hi.'

'No, don't! Another time . . .' I bite my lip. There will be no other time. Soon there will be no more Ryan in my life either. I take a deep breath and hurry over to Dad.

Ryan looks puzzled but gives him a wave. Dad forces his lips upwards and waves back at Ryan as he catches hold of my arm. I can feel his vice-like fingers digging into my skin. He doesn't look at me.

'Consider him dumped,' he says quietly, nodding pleasantly to Ryan, and giving him another wave before hurrying me back through the crowd towards the path to the caravan site. And I know he's furious because he's not telling me off. He doesn't say a word. Suddenly a voice I recognise rings out from behind us.

'Mr Smith, I presume?'

Surprised, Dad looks around as the familiar shape of Miss Turner steps out of the darkness.

'Turner, Miss Turner,' she tells him. 'I spoke to you earlier today on the phone?'

'Oh yes. Of course.' He assumes charming mode, flashes a huge smile and says, 'Nice to meet you.'

'And you too.'

'What a fantastic concert – and for such a good cause! What would we do without the lifeboats, eh?'

'Absolutely . . . Not staying then?'

He gives a disappointed sigh. 'Grace isn't feeling too good. Are you, love?'

I shake my head.

'What a shame.' Miss Turner is staring hard at me now. A wave of nausea floods up from my churning stomach. I must look awful.

'A good night's sleep and she'll be right as rain,' Dad says warmly.

'Course. So I'll see your wife tomorrow.'

His eyes flick between her and me, and I can detect the suspicion in them. 'I hear Gracie has been in a spot of trouble?' he says letting go of my arm and putting his around my shoulder.

'Grace and I have had one or two problems since she arrived, but there are several things I want to discuss.' Miss Turner looks him straight in the eye, but like a poker player, gives nothing away.

Dad pulls a face. 'I'm afraid that may not be possible after all. You see we're leaving tomorrow.'

'Leaving?' Miss Turner looks surprised. 'I wasn't aware you were leaving! This is a complete surprise.'

'It's totally unexpected for us too. We had hoped to move down here permanently, but it's just not going to happen. My new job's fallen through. The girls are gutted – we all are – but that's the way it goes.'

'All the more reason for your wife to pop in then. I'll inform the Head and we can sort out the transfer paperwork for their next school.'

'I'm not sure we'll have time – there's a lot to pack and —'

'It won't take long and it'll give the girls a chance to say goodbye to all their friends.' She darts a look at Dad. 'Unless you have a problem with that?'

The corner of Dad's mouth twitches but he pushes his smile still wider.

'Goodness, no . . . That's fine! Absolutely fine! I'm sure we'll fit everything in.'

'See you tomorrow in registration, Grace,' she tells me with an authoritative nod as Dad hurries me off.

'You've said something, haven't you?' he hisses at me when we're out of earshot, digging his fingers into my shoulder. 'Haven't you?'

I shake my head violently. He increases his pace half pulling me along.

'It was your sister then, wasn't it? Telling tales. I might have known she couldn't keep her big mouth shut.'

Chapter 59

Ellie

Dad bursts into the caravan pulling Grace behind him like a rag doll.

He snatches Grandad's violin from her hand and smashes it against the hard metal of the cooker, splintering it into pieces, then snaps the bow over his thigh and chucks it on top of the quilt lying in the corner.

We stare at him shocked. Tears well up in Grace's eyes but she doesn't dare move to pick anything up. None of us move. Bruno starts to whimper. Even the caravan shudders as the wind blows around it.

'One word out of place tomorrow,' Dad snarls, as he grabs Bruno's collar and heaves him outside. 'Just one single word and I'll kill you,' he threatens Mum. He turns to Grace and me. 'Do you hear that? Are you listening?'

Grace mouths and I say, 'Yes, Dad.'

'Now get out of my sight!'

We hurry into our little bedroom and close the door behind us. I don't ask Grace what happened. I don't need to. She sits on the little bunk shaking. I put my arm around her and whisper that everything is going to be OK, but I don't believe the words as I force them out of my mouth and I can't stop her trembling however hard I hug her.

We don't sleep. We wait. We listen. We hope and we pray Mum is OK in the other room. Outside I can hear Bruno whining gently to come back inside. Quietly, I open our window, lean out and stretch my hand down to him. He puts his paws up on the side of the caravan. I whisper reassuring words to him as he licks my fingers then finally lies down to sleep under our room, out of the wind.

When it gets light, we dress for school. Mum and Dad are already up. Mum is wearing her black trousers and a high-necked, long-sleeved blouse. Feeling too sick to eat breakfast we head off to school.

I've just got to my first lesson, when I'm summoned to Miss Turner's office. Everyone turns and stares at me as I hurry out of class, wondering what's going on.

I step into her room and see Mum sitting in front of the desk, nervously clutching her handbag on her lap. Seconds later Grace comes in, followed by Mad Mulligan and Miss Turner.

Mad Mulligan gives me a thin smile as I sit down but I daren't look at her. My heart's pounding as I realise she's taken what I said about Dad seriously.

Miss Turner starts talking when suddenly the door swings open and Dad walks in.

'Oh . . . I thought my wife was just picking up paperwork,' he says in a jolly tone. 'This looks much more serious!'

'Why don't you join us, Mr Smith?' asks Miss Turner, glancing at me. 'I think Ellie has something she wants to say.'

He turns to me, shaking his head. 'Oh Lord! So that's what all this is about. I might have known. Ellie, I give up!'

I freeze. I daren't say a word.

'I'm sorry?' asks Miss Turner.

'We are having *so* much trouble at home with Ellie at the moment, aren't we, love?'

He turns to Mum and looks at her. She nods.

'It's very embarrassing to admit this, Miss Turner, but putting it bluntly, Ellie tells lies. Great big whoppers. We have tried, haven't we, Karin? Oh, we've tried everything, but it's compulsive. Do you know, she swore blind at her last school that she was adopted! Broke your heart, didn't she, love?'

All eyes are on Mum again. She nods. 'It was . . . upsetting.'

'Confidentially, we've even seen our GP. He said she'll grow out of it. We're still waiting!' He lowers his voice and appeals to Miss Turner. 'Look, I know we're leaving, and it's all a bit late now, but I think Karin and I, well, we'd both appreciate any professional advice you can give us, Miss Turner – anything that could help, because frankly we're at our wits end, aren't we, love?'

As Mum nods, Dad turns to me and asks wearily, 'So, Ellie, what have you said this time?'

'Um . . . nothing . . .' I mumble.

'Come on Ellie, spit it out.'

Although I don't look at him I can feel his eyes boring into me. There's a deathly silence. Everyone's looking at me now. I glance at Mum, remembering Dad's horrible threats about killing her.

'I . . . I told everyone you were an actor in America,' I mumble.

Dad bursts out laughing.

'Oh, Ellie, for goodness' sake!' He rolls his eyes at Miss Turner and says, 'I'm an accountant. I work in an office. Well, I suppose that's less serious than her usual lurid tales.'

'Ellie has also made other accusations,' says Miss Turner. 'Serious accusations that as a school we have a duty to investigate, whether you're leaving or not.'

'Accusations? Really? Well . . . that doesn't surprise me. You can see what we're up against.' Dad shakes his head.

'She's frightened of you,' says Mad Mulligan.

'Oh come on, Ellie, really!' Dad protests with a laugh.

'She says you can be violent and aggressive.'

'Me? Violent? You must be joking! Now that's not funny, Ellie. Karin, can you believe it?'

Mum shakes her head and Dad carries on.

'You've really gone too far now, Ellie. Miss Turner, I can tell you exactly what this is all about. If I tell you off for something, Ellie, you can't get your revenge by going around making me out to be some kind of monster! This has got to stop. Right now. Before you get yourself in real trouble. Do you understand?' There's an edge in his voice that I know well.

I glance at Mum, and see the desperation behind her blank expression.

'Look, I'll admit it. I am strict – too strict, some people might say,' Dad says with a glance at Mad Mulligan. 'But let's face it, kids today, kids like Ellie, need a firm hand – they'll run wild otherwise, but they'll thank you for it when they're older. But as to being violent? That's a complete and utter pack of lies. Tell them, Karin.'

All eyes are on Mum.

'Perhaps it would be better if you spoke to us without your husband present?' asks Turner.

'I don't mind,' Dad says. 'Absolutely no problem. D'you want me to wait outside, Karin?'

'No it's OK . . .' Mum says. 'Miss Turner, Ellie is a very imaginative girl, and I suppose her imagination runs away with her sometimes. She doesn't mean it but that's what happens. But apart from that, everything's fine at home. Really. There's nothing wrong.'

'Ellie, if you are just telling tales, you'll be in one hell of a lot of trouble,' Miss Turner warns me.

I look over at Dad. He's smiling at us because he knows he's won.

Chapter 60

Grace

My mouth is as dry as sandpaper. I swallow hard but a jagged lump sticks halfway down my throat adding to the choking sensation already there. My stomach churns angrily and although I'm feeling dizzy, I force the soles of my feet into the floor and push myself up.

'Grace?' asks Mrs Mulligan, seeing me swaying slightly. 'Are you all right?'

'Ellie's telling the truth,' I hear a voice whisper.

'Grace . . .' Mum says.

I realise the whisper was mine.

'Mum. No more.'

'No . . . Grace, don't . . .'

'We have to tell them what it's like walking on eggshells all the time.'

'Please, love . . .'

My voice becomes louder and clearer with every word. It's as if I'm waking up.

'We have to explain how terrified we were, so we drove through the night to get away from him. They have to know we needed to be safe. And if we don't speak now, if we don't tell, it's going to happen all over again.'

Miss Turner stares at me, astonished.

'This is ludicrous!' Dad blusters. 'I've never heard such a load of rubbish in all my life. Grace, what has got into you?'

'Looks like she's found her voice,' Miss Turner says. 'This is the first time Grace has spoken to a teacher in school and now I think I understand why.'

'Oh come on!' he remonstrates. 'You don't seriously believe her, do you?'

Miss Turner takes out a purple patterned notebook from her bag. 'Ellie left this in the hall after she spoke to Mrs Mulligan, who kindly handed it to me. I have read it from cover to cover. The content is most illuminating. Ellie, show me your right arm and tell me what happened.'

Darting a frightened glance at Dad, Ellie rolls up her sleeve and reveals the bruising.

'An accident! That was just an accident!' Dad shouts angrily. 'This is ridiculous!'

Everyone's staring at Ellie now. She shrinks back slightly and bites her lip before glancing at me.

'Tell them,' I urge her.

'You threw your mug of tea at me,' Ellie says, looking Dad in the eye.

'You are in one big load of trouble, Drama Queenie, making up these stories,' he retorts angrily. 'You wait till we get home.'

'No,' says Mum quietly, shaking her head.

'What d'you mean, "no"?'

'We're not coming home, Adam,' says Mum firmly.

'What?'

'It's over.'

'Karin, think about what you're doing.'

'I am. The girls are right. I should have spoken up long ago but you frightened me so much I didn't have the courage. We've made a new life here without you and this is where we're staying.'

Dad's face changes, his mouth twists up into a horrible snarl.

'Fine!' he snaps. 'Suits me. I'm finished with you. You can go to hell, the lot of you.'

He leaps up and flies out of the room, barging past Miss Turner.

Mum looks like she's going to burst into tears. Mad Mulligan puts her arm around her but she shakes her head.

'I'm all right. Thank you. For the first time. I'm all right.'

'What about Dad?' Ellie asks fearfully.

'Mrs Mulligan, would you ring Mr Nesbit please and get him to check Mr Smith has left the premises, then take the girls to your office for a while. I want to talk to the Headmaster with your mother and then we need to make some phone calls.'

Chapter 61

Ellie

We spend an hour in Mad Mulligan's office then Miss Turner comes in and takes us back to our classes. She tells us that Mum is going to be busy for the next few hours and we'd be best carrying on as normal in school. As if. The last things on my mind are oxbow lakes and French verbs. Cait wants to know what happened but I'm too upset to tell her much.

I burst into tears halfway through the dress rehearsal at lunchtime and Mad Mulligan lets me sit in her office for the rest of the day and work quietly there. Grace is already there. We huddle at her desk with our books in front of us, staring fearfully through the window at the sunshine outside, wondering where Dad is. At three-thirty Mum is waiting for us at the gate with Bruno and a lady called Lisa who explains that she's from the women's refuge and she's going to be supporting Mum.

Mum gives me an encouraging nod so I say hello, but Grace looks warily down the street.

'It's OK. He's gone,' says Mum. 'He's taken his stuff from the caravan and picked up the car from the garage.'

'But he knows where we are.'

230

'Lisa's son is a mechanic at the garage,' Mum tells us. 'When Dad picked up the car, he watched him drive off and take the London road.'

'But what if he comes back next week or something?'

'We're going to have to move. Lisa thinks it's best if we stay at the refuge tonight, then she's going to help me sort things out first thing tomorrow,' Mum tells us. 'We're going to look at a couple of places in town that we might be able to rent. Don't worry. Everything's going to be OK.'

'Do you want me to come back with you?' Lisa asks.

'No, we'll be all right. We'll just grab our stuff and go.'

'OK, see you in an hour or so. You've got my number, if you need me.'

'Thanks . . . for everything,' Mum tells her.

We hurry back home. A sea mist is rolling in and we can hear the low rumble of thunder from far away.

Back at the caravan, most of the flowers Mum had planted around the front have been trampled and a few have been ripped out of the earth and thrown onto the grass. Mum warns us that there's a bit of a mess inside.

'I didn't want you both to see all this but I just didn't have time to sort it out, what with everything else.'

Grace and I step in the caravan and look around, dismayed. This morning our bags had been neatly packed, ready to be put in the car when we left this evening. Now, everything has been pulled out, chucked everywhere, ripped or stamped on or trashed.

'Let's just throw everything back in the bags and go,' Mum says pulling a face as she puts the caravan keys and her mobile down on the table. 'We can sort it all out at the refuge.'

'I don't think so,' says a voice.

I jump in shock as my blood runs cold. Dad is standing in the open doorway his arms stretched up to the top of the frame like bars on a cage. Grace and I freeze but Mum steps protectively in front of us. Outside, Bruno barks. Dad turns and snaps at him to shut up or else, then orders him into the caravan. With his tail down between his legs he reluctantly obeys.

'I want you to go, Adam. Now,' Mum tells Dad in a clear but trembling voice as he steps inside.

'Oh, I'm going all right. But in my own time. I'm the boss of you – and don't you ever forget it. You don't tell me what to do. In fact, you don't tell me anything any more.'

He picks up Mum's phone and snatches the caravan keys from the table.

Mum attempts to stop him but he punches her with his fist. With blood running from her nose, she reels back against the wall making the whole caravan shudder. Groaning and dazed, she tries to get to her feet.

'Get out!' Grace screams at him as I run to help Mum.

He turns and steps out of the caravan. Grace tries to shut the door on him but he forces it open with his foot, pushing her away. Picking up a large rusty can, he pours what looks like dirty water over the carpet inside.

As a horrid petrol smell hits me, he clicks on a lighter and tosses it into the air above the soaked carpet, which becomes a wall of flames, then he quickly slams the door shut. Grace grabs the handle, frantically trying to push open the door as we hear the key rattle in the lock.

I try to stamp out the flames but it's hopeless as within seconds they've spread and black smoke is starting to engulf the van. The smoke alarm is screeching madly. Bruno leaps about terrified. As Mum staggers to her feet, I dive at the window, and wrestle with the catch, but it won't open.

Grace tries another window.

'They're locked!' I yell thumping on the glass. 'We can't get out!'

Outside we see Susan, appearing from her caravan then rushing over as she realises something's wrong. I shout and scream. Bruno's barking madly, but Grace picks up the quilt from the floor. She wraps it around her feet and bracing herself against the back of the bench seat, kicks furiously against the window.

'Ellie, help me!' she yells.

I sit next to her and we kick hard until suddenly the window gives, and a fierce cold wind rushes in, feeding and fanning the flames.

'Quickly!'

Coughing and spluttering, we half drag, half pull Mum over to the window and help her through it before climbing out after her onto the grass. Bruno springs out too and runs off. I call to him to stop but my voice is lost in the wind. The whole van is engulfed in bright orange flames now.

'Are you all right?' Mum asks.

'We're OK,' Grace tells her as Susan calls nine-nine-nine on her mobile.

As Bruno disappears up the path towards the stones, I set off after him.

'Ellie! Wait!' Grace calls, catching me up. 'I saw Dad run up that way,' she tells me.

'I don't care,' I shout back as we see a huge streak of lightning spike down ahead of us. 'Bruno's petrified. I've got to get him.'

'I'm coming with you,' she says.

We get to the stone circle just as a terrific crash of thunder sounds. Bruno is cowering against the tallest Maid, his eyes wide with fear. The hairs on the back of my neck stand on end and I can sense the tingling of electricity in the air as another bolt of lightning fires angrily down from the sky.

'It's OK,' I tell Bruno, crouching down next to him, stroking him gently.

Suddenly I'm being yanked up from behind by a dark shadow. I turn to see Dad. I scream, struggling madly, but he's caught me tight. Grace runs over and batters his back with her fists, trying to make him loosen his grip on me.

As he spins around to snatch her too, I jab my elbows into him and kick out as hard as I can. He yells with rage, letting go of me for a second. Grace and I dive around the back of the Maid. He swears angrily, determined to grab us as the tall stone creaks, wobbling like a loose tooth. There's a yell from Grace who pulls me backwards as the stone suddenly topples.

Instead of trying to get out of its way, Dad irritably tries to push it to one side but it's much heavier than he thinks. The stone crashes against him, pushing him to the ground, pinning him down. Blood seeps through his shirt, staining it bright red.

'Dad!' I yell.

There's no reply. I'm convinced he's dead until I see a few of his fingers twitch slightly and hear him groan. He's hurt, badly. I squat down and try to lift the huge rock, but it's way too heavy.

'Grace, help me!' I shout.

She hesitates for a second then kneels beside me and together we lift the stone off him.

Grace pulls off her school jumper, rolls it up and gently puts it under his head. 'We need to get help.'

As if in answer, we hear sirens, becoming louder by the second. We stare at him, alarmed as his eyes open, wide with fear.

'It's all right. Keep still,' I tell him as he breathes heavily.

I take his hand and hold it in mine. And I'm confused because it's soft and white and flabby, not at all like the hard fist that used to punch and hit Mum.

Chapter 62

Grace

In the end we don't need to go for help. Help comes to us. Mum first.

Ellie bursts into tears when she sees her. 'Why does he hate us so much?' she asks, as Mum checks Dad's pulse. His eyes are closed and he seems to be unconscious.

'I don't know, sweetheart,' she says.

'But what have we ever done to him to make him so angry all the time?'

'Nothing. You've done nothing.'

'Then why?'

Dad opens his eyes. 'He used to hit me,' he mutters.

Mum, Ellie and I look at each other, confused.

'Who?' Ellie asks.

The lids of his eyes slowly close and nothing happens for a long time. Finally his lips move. No words come out at first and we keep sitting in silence. Then he gives a kind of shudder and speaks hoarsely. 'I'd hide but he'd always find me. She'd tell him where I was.'

'Who hit you, Dad?' Ellie asks again.

'My dad.' He whispers it so quietly we can barely hear him.

A lump comes to my throat. We never knew this. Dad always said he'd had the perfect parents. Why didn't he tell us the truth? I look at Mum – did she know? Her face tells me not. Tears are streaking down her cheeks, washing away the blood and grime.

'You could have been different with us, Adam,' she says. 'You had a choice. You didn't have to tell the same story.'

He doesn't reply but lies helplessly in front of us as four policemen arrive, one armed with what looks like a gun. They tell us to step away from Dad and shout warnings at him not to move or they'll use their taser.

'He can't – he's hurt,' Ellie says but they don't listen. We're quickly ushered away and taken back to the field. We stand at a distance, watching the firemen put out the flames of our burning caravan. Someone puts Gran's quilt, battered and dirty, around our shoulders. Mum, Ellie and I huddle under it with Bruno, shivering in the rain as the storm rumbles off into the distance.

Stan arrives and Mum tells him she's sorry for what's happened.

'I should have done more,' he mutters, shaking his head. 'Right from when I first saw you, I had a gut feeling something was wrong. Didn't like to interfere, see. That's the trouble. Too busy minding my own business.'

'It's not your fault,' Mum tells him.

'No, but I might have been able to help. The more people who know what's going on, the better.'

Susan takes us back to her caravan where she and one of the police officers make us hot drinks. We sit sipping mugs of tea sweetened with honey, answering his questions as the rain rattles down on the roof. An hour later he drives us down to the police station where we tell our story once more and answer more questions and the same questions all over again.

It's late when Stan arrives. Mum thanks him and tells him we can go to the women's refuge but he insists that we come home with him and stay the night there. Mum rings the refuge and explains what's happened, then Stan drives us back to his house where Daphne is waiting. She hugs each of us in turn, makes a fuss of Bruno then takes Ellie and I into one spare bedroom and shows Mum to another.

I don't realise how exhausted I am until my head hits the pillow. I look over at Ellie but she's already fast asleep.

When I wake, my watch says it's gone lunchtime but I can smell bacon frying. Ellie's still asleep so I try to get out of bed really quietly but she hears me and opens her eyes. With a puzzled expression, she glances down at the long pink nightie she's wearing then does a double take at me wearing a similar one in pale blue. Outside in the garden, drying in the wind, gran's quilt is pegged on the washing line, together with the clothes we were wearing last night.

'You OK?' I ask Ellie.

As she slowly nods, there's a tap on the door. It's Mum. She's wearing one of Daphne's dressing gowns, a fleecy creation in pale yellow.

'There's someone here to see us,' she says quietly.

I exchange looks with Ellie, thinking we're going to have to answer yet more questions, when a face I instantly recognise appears behind Mum.

'Auntie Anna!' Ellie exclaims.

'Karin phoned me early this morning. I jumped in the car and drove straight here,' she explains, giving us both a hug. 'Thank God you're all right.'

Daphne calls us into a sunny dining room where a table is laid for breakfast. We all sit down together to eat and talk for the next couple of hours.

Mum tells Anna she's sorry for not staying in touch and bursts into tears. Anna hugs her and starts crying too, telling her she's got nothing to be sorry for, she should have done more – that they were sisters and always would be. Soon we're all crying except Stan who just noisily blows his nose a couple of times into a big white hanky then disappears into the kitchen saying he'll make more coffee.

Once Mum has told Auntie Anna everything that has happened, they start to talk about happier times, when they came here on holiday with Gran and Grandad. They tell us about seal watching and the picnics on the beach, toasting marshmallows over a little driftwood campfire, and the daft talent contest in town that Mum and Anna won, singing together in their matching pink dresses, until no one's crying any more and the room's full of laughter.

Chapter 63

Ellie

Anna tells Mum she'll take the week off and stay with us. We spend the rest of the day at Stan and Daphne's house. School isn't even mentioned. Late in the afternoon, Mum and Anna go out for a couple of hours and when they come back, Mum announces that with Lisa's help they've found a small, furnished cottage for us to rent and we're moving in that evening.

Daphne and Stan come with us, bringing carrier bags full of food and practical stuff like shampoo, soap and toothbrushes. Lisa turns up an hour later with bedding, towels and a bag of clothes from the refuge, as we have nothing but the things we were wearing yesterday and Gran's quilt. Everything else has been burnt in the fire.

There are two bedrooms upstairs in the little cottage, a downstairs bathroom behind the kitchen and a cosy sitting room. It doesn't take us long to unpack the few bits and pieces and make ourselves at home. Anna and Mum hang up the quilt in the sitting room, where it covers most of one wall. Bruno sniffs around all the rooms and then stretches out happily on the rug in the sitting room, in front of the wood-burner. After living in a cramped caravan for so many weeks this tiny cottage seems like a mansion.

The next day, Grace and I go back to school, the smoke and grime washed out of our school uniforms. As we walk through the school gates, Grace sees Ryan and hurries over to him. I spot Cait chatting with Abs, Ruby, Shareen and Freya. When she sees me, she waves frantically and they all run over.

'Are you OK?' Abs asks. 'We heard all sorts of stuff.'

I nod. 'Thanks to Cait. She made me tell Mulligan about my dad.'

'Did he really torch your caravan?' asks Shareen.

I nod slowly, as it finally sinks in that Dad actually tried to kill us.

'You must have been terrified,' says Ruby.

'It was horrible,' I reply.

'What's going to happen to him?' Abs asks.

'He's in hospital with broken ribs and stuff but the police are going to arrest him.'

'Are you ever going to see him again?' asks Freya.

'I don't know. I'm not sure I want to. Not after what he's done.'

'But you're not going back to London now, are you?'

'No, we're staying here. We moved into a little cottage in town last night.'

'That's great,' Cait says.

'Yeah, we'd really miss you if you left, wouldn't we?' adds Ruby, and the others all agree.

'I'm really sorry I told you lot so many lies,' I say, not daring to look at them.

'You should have told us what was really going on. We're your mates,' Abs tells me.

'I know. I'm sorry.' I hang my head. 'I was ashamed and embarrassed. Still am.'

'It isn't your fault!' protests Shareen. 'You aren't to blame!'

'I used to think I was, but I know better now.'

The bell rings and we head into school together, passing PJ in the corridor who gives us the evils.

'I dumped him yesterday,' Cait whispers to me. 'You were so right, Ellie. My next boyfriend is going to make me laugh, not laugh at me all the time.' She pauses for a moment then adds, 'What do you think of Kev in Ryan's band?'

Chapter 64

Grace

'Are you OK?' asks Ryan. 'Mrs Woollacott told Dad someone set your caravan on fire. What happened?'

I tell him the whole story. He listens, shocked.

'You should have told me about your dad before,' he says finally.

'I know. The stupid thing was, I didn't trust anyone.'

'But you trust me, now?'

'Completely.'

He leans towards me to kiss me. I really do go weak at the knees, like you're supposed to.

'Ryan Baxter, that's quite enough of that!' barks a voice behind us. It's Miss Turner. Ryan ignores her and finishes kissing me.

'Zero tolerance dictates that I should put you both in detention this afternoon,' Turner snaps. 'But under the circumstances, you are excused.' Her voice softens. 'How are you, Grace?'

'I'm OK, Miss, thanks,' I reply.

'It's good to have you back. Never like to see a pupil slip

through my net. Now. You know exactly where my office is. You make sure you come straight to me if there's something wrong in future. Understand?'

'Yes, Miss.'

'I mean it. They might call me the old rottweiler, but I'm the old rottweiler who's on your side. And I have very sharp teeth. Remember that.'

'Thanks, Miss.'

'Miss Turner.'

Thanks, Miss Turner.'

'There's hope for you yet,' she says walking past us into school.

And she's right. There is hope. Day by day, things do get better until I no longer get that horrible churning in my stomach or clam up when I want to talk to someone. I'm making up for lost time; Ellie moaned at lunch-break yesterday that she can't get a word in edgeways now and told me to put a cork in it. She sounded quite cross, although I think it's nerves – it's the first performance of *Princess Caraboo* tonight and Auntie Anna is staying on especially to watch. We've got seats for Stan, Daphne and Susan too, and Ryan's going to be watching with his dad and the twins.

I stay on after school with Ellie to help with the costumes. As the time of the performance gets closer, tension is running high backstage. Mad Mulligan's the worst culprit, shrieking at everyone and throwing a hissy fit every few minutes. Finally the moment arrives, the hall's packed, and the audience are sitting, waiting in anticipation as the music begins.

'Good luck,' I whisper to Ellie as she waits in the wings for her cue on stage.

She turns and looks at me with panic in her eyes.

'Gracie, I'm so nervous!' she replies, her voice shaking. 'I never thought I would be – but I'm terrified. What if I forget my words or freeze up?'

'You won't,' I reassure her. 'Everything's going to be all right.'

'How do you know?' she asks anxiously.

I look her straight in the eyes. 'You've got nothing to hide any more.'

A smile spreads across her face. She nods, takes a deep breath, then strides out on stage.

Nominated for the Carnegie Medal

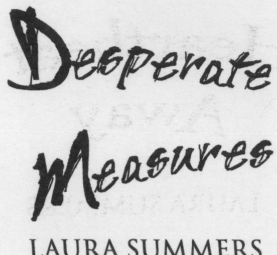

Desperate Measures

LAURA SUMMERS

Vicky and Rhianna are twins but they couldn't
be more different. On their fourteenth birthday,
they get a nasty shock.

Their foster parents can't cope and it looks
as if Vicky and Rhianna and their younger
brother Jamie will have to be split up.

How can they stay together?
Desperate times call for desperate measures . . .

'An exciting adventure with plenty of drama
and humour . . . Thought-provoking and moving.'
Books for Keeps

'A fabulous book . . . incredibly poignant.'
Birmingham Post

Heartbeat
Away

LAURA SUMMERS

Becky's getting stronger by the day after her
heart transplant, but soon she starts
to have disturbing experiences.

Vivid pictures of unfamiliar people and places suddenly
flash through her mind. What can they mean?
Drawn to a park on the far side of town,
Becky begins to unravel a mystery
deeply buried in her new heart.

'A mystery with a hint of the paranormal . . .
Laura Summers proves she's a distinctive and original voice.'
The Bookseller

DO YOU BELIEVE IN DESTINY?

I'LL BE THERE

HOLLY GOLDBERG SLOAN

Everyone whose path you cross in life
has the power to change you.

Emily believes in destiny. She's been waiting
for the moment her real life begins.

Sam wishes he could escape. He's spent his life being
dragged from place to place by his father.
But he could never abandon his little brother.

Then everything changes. Because Sam meets Emily.

This tender story of star-crossed love is both romance
and thriller, and a compelling exploration
of the power of human connection.

'Heartbreaking, suspenseful, life-affirming, magical.'
Gayle Forman

piccadillypress.co.uk/teen

Go online to discover:

☆ more great books you'll love

☆ competitions

☆ sneak peeks inside books

☆ fun activities, trailers and downloads

☆ author interviews

☆ and much more!